THE
INTERNET
PEDOPHILE
IS *HERE*

THE INTERNET PEDOPHILE IS *HERE*

NANA MUMFORD

The Internet Pedophile Is Here
Copyright © 2020 by Nana Mumford. All rights reserved.

No part of this publication may be reproduced, stored in a retrieval system or transmitted in any way by any means, electronic, mechanical, photocopy, recording or otherwise without the prior permission of the author except as provided by USA copyright law.

The opinions expressed by the author are not necessarily those of URLink Print and Media.

1603 Capitol Ave., Suite 310 Cheyenne, Wyoming USA 82001
1-888-980-6523 | admin@urlinkpublishing.com

URLink Print and Media is committed to excellence in the publishing industry.

Book design copyright © 2020 by URLink Print and Media. All rights reserved.

Published in the United States of America

Library of Congress Control Number: 2020901277
ISBN 978-1-64753-181-2 (Paperback)
ISBN 978-1-64753-182-9 (Digital)

17.03.20

CONTENTS

Dedication And Acknowledgement 7
Introduction 9
1. Holidaying at Del Soro 11
2. Life in Metropolisia Cosma 16
3. Professionals Behaving Madly 26
4. Beastly Neighborhood 38
5. Topsy-turvy Relationships 50
6. Cosma Crown Court 67
7. Glib Talk 91
8. Cosma Secure Unit-Treatment Sessions 104
9. Wednesday Session 127
10. Thursday Session 135
11. Friday Session 144
12. The Eye of The Hawk 152
13. Electronic Reconnaissance 164
14. The Last Sense 177
15. Grand Finale 194

DEDICATION AND ACKNOWLEDGEMENT

This book is dedicated to Ava, Ezra, Zadok, and Romeo, who are found to be far more valuable than the best of diamonds, virtuous, of noble character and fear God.

I wish to express my sincere gratefulness to the personnel at the Internet Watch Foundation in Oakington, UK, especially David Kerr, for giving me audience and providing me with vital information. I also thank Jim Reynolds and Peter Spindler of the National Crime Squad, London, Terry Jones of Greater Manchester Police, the Obscene Publications Unit and various Internet Service Providers for their invaluable contribution. My acknowledgement would not be complete without mentioning Lori Scott, former Senior Probation Officer with the Sex Offender Team in the Adult Probation Department of Maricopa County in Phoenix, Arizona. She, in liaison with the Phoenix Probation Department, afforded me a great opportunity to obtain vital information.

Most of the factors underlying Internet pedophilia, raised in the book, were confirmed during major international conferences I attended (Internet Content Summit, Munich, September 9-11, 1999; Dealing with Paedophilia and the Sexual Exploitation of Children, The Barbican Centre, London, 6 December 2000; Safe Internet Surfing Conference, Singapore, 20-26 February, 2001; Child Pornography and the Internet, The Barbican Centre, London, 18 September 2001; International conference in Vancouver, Canada in February 2002). I met many practitioners and policy makers in the problem areas of the Internet, who consented to throw further light on the issues involved, and thus became sources of information.

I wish to thank the organizers of these international conferences, through whose efforts I managed to learn a lot from like-minded scholars and obtained vital data, which otherwise would have been found no where else.

INTRODUCTION

Didn't he have the right to take a holiday? Didn't he have the right to complete protection on such a holiday? Elijah Morrison, an oil executive from Calgary, Canada, and his family had all these rights. But when he ventured to Del Soro, an Island in the Mediterranean Sea, disaster struck, as their four-year old daughter, Elsie, was abducted, raped and unimaginable pornographic images recorded of the ordeal she went through.

However, Elijah was somehow fortunate. He had a chance encounter with a mysterious being, the Revealer, who opened his eyes in a spectacular vision to learn of the profile of the perpetrator of his daughter's ordeal.

Assuming different roles, he was made to come face to face with many typical Internet pedophiles. His portfolio was to challenge the mentality of such beings. You cannot imagine what he saw and heard.

It took the normal forensic evidence and the paranormal of a vision he had of the murderer, to execute justice in both Calgary and Del Soro. Take your seat with the author, Nana Mumford, relax, put yourself in Elijah's shoes and pose as many of your own challenging questions as possible to these creatures as you read.

CHAPTER ONE

HOLIDAYING AT DEL SORO

Elijah Morrison was a well-known charismatic family man in a vibrant Calgary community, who exuded hope and confidence in those who interacted with him, both socially and professionally. He was an executive director of Karaka Oil Company in Calgary, Canada. However, after his four-year old daughter was abducted, raped and killed, he became very withdrawn and he was often seen spending more time praying either in the local Pentecostal church or one of the quiet resorts along the Bow River. When his daughter's body was found in the cave about a mile from their holiday resort and it was realized, after intensive search that horrendous pornographic images of her were also recorded detailing the extent of sexual abuse she suffered, public reaction against pedophiles both on the Island and in Calgary was overwhelming. Elijah's mind went as far back as he could to ascertain if he had any problems with the people he dealt with in his business. Was it an issue with any particular religious group? Did he deal unfairly with any racial group? Any younger or older man who bore him a grudge? Was it a random meeting with a murderer on the Island? He thought about why he had to meet such a fate.

Suddenly, he remembered that three years prior to this trip, he abrogated a deal to be supplied with pipelines from a ruthless sub-contractor, a Canadian of Asian origin, Chen Ping. It emerged that the contractor's pipelines from an Asian manufacturing company were of inferior quality. Quality control checks on these pipes found microscopic holes in them, rendering them liable to seepages. Not only that. A later background check on him indicated that he had connections with the Russian Mafia and may be selling the pipelines at throat-cutting prices. Apparently, the disappointment did not go down well with Chen Ping. It became known to Elijah later that his business went bust and nearly committed suicide. He survived after early intervention. Thereafter, he went silent. Was he the one who might have perpetrated this evil against him? Time will tell.

"How did it all start?" he asked himself. After so many months of hard work and hardly seeing his family for any length of time, Bertha, his wife appealed to him to have a break and go away for awhile with the family, including Elsie Morrison, their four old daughter and Jojo, their six-year old son. After tying loose ends in his business deals, they took a four-week holiday to the tiny Island of Del Soro, in the middle of the Mediterranean Sea. As an oil tycoon, he could afford a 3-bedroom flat set on the slopes of one of the two hills on the Island.

It was three weeks into their holiday, Saturday night, July 10th, the eve of the Island's national holiday. Del Soro has been known traditionally as a children's paradise, when on such occasions children's bazaars are held over the Island and parties are held for them till about 2 am the following day. That Saturday, Elijah Morrison, Bertha, Jojo and Elsie were on the party trail. They arrived at home at about 3 am Sunday tired. After the usual facial washes and toiletries, they reposed to bed. The master bedroom was occupied by the couple and the kids occupied the two other rooms each. Being a bit hot and stuffy, the windows were not locked in all the bedrooms. Who would have thought that on this holiday on a friendly Island with insignificant crime statistics, any sinister act would be committed? The family woke up at about 10 am to a bright day, and Mr and Mrs Morrison looked through the window, which overlooked a beautiful beach. Elijah told Bertha, "God is good all the time."

Bertha responded, "All the time God is good."

As they went to the living room, they met Jojo smiling.

"Dad, Mum are you alright?"

"Yea, and you and Elsie?"

"Oh Dad, I have not seen or heard of Elsie and I thought she was with you."

They all rushed to her bedroom. She was not there.

"Bertha, check the kitchen and the garden, while I look under her bed," Elijah directed. It was becoming alarming, as all search yielded nothing.

"Lord have mercy," as Bertha started to cry.

They called the police, and despite frantic search for her in their last week of the holiday, Elsie could not be found. They decided to inform Elijah's company in Calgary in order for them to stay on for as long as it took to cooperate with the police until it became necessary to abandon the search, if she was not found. But the situation was so unbearable that they flew back to Canada early morning the following Friday. Their problem compounded when rumours were going round that the couple may have killed their daughter and pretending. It was on the same day, Friday, around 4 pm in one of the caves at the beach that a nearly decomposed body of a girl was found. Forensic tests conducted later on the body indicted that it was Elsie's. The family received the news with shock and were in profound grief.

One Sunday at 2:30 pm in the fall of that year, Elijah went to one of the resorts along the Bow River as usual to meditate on recent events and to come to terms with the family's loss. The usual thoughts came back to haunt him once again. Who could have done this to us? Could this person be of a special religious background? Is he an enemy from a particular racial background? Did we fall prey to criminals of a particular socio-cultural background? He was thinking about what sort of person may have committed this evil against his family and what could be the reasons.

And as he looked into the sky, and the waves beat incessantly at the rocks beneath him, he fell into a trance. The experience he detailed later was incredible. A wall appeared before him and the date inscribed on it was 6 June 6666: Welcome to the Isle of Metropolisia Cosma: The Land of Interpeds.

He spoke to himself, "this is an unusual year. It is well into the future. Numerically, today is 666666, double the mark of the beast. Surely, there must be something doubly sinister on this land, which I am about to see, and what is Interpeds?"

Suddenly, he heard a thundering voice saying: "Elijah, Elijah, Interpeds is short for Internet pedophiles. Now behold the number of people standing before you." Elijah became petrified when he heard the strange voice.

"Who are you?" he questioned.

"I am the Revealer. You will get to know me better with time," the voice responded. There were 251 beings draped completely from head to toe in crimson red dresses, with the exception of their eyes.

"Who are these beings coming in my direction, Revealer?" Elijah wanted to know.

"They have one thing in common: to feed on the nakedness of children. They have just had their dinner and are on their way for a dessert. Pedophilia is how they describe this sickening behaviour that used to be conducted within the walls of certain so-called social elites, where it was considered a rarity to be enjoyed discreetly yet in excessively insatiable way. This phenomenon has been the fear of societies for a long time. But it has come out of its closet in another form in this age of advanced technology."

Elijah exclaimed, "Uh!"

The voice thundered, "Elijah, Elijah, open your eyes widely for what I am about to reveal to you."

In his vision, Elijah started crying as the scene unfolded before his very eyes.

CHAPTER TWO

LIFE IN METROPOLISIA COSMA

With trepidation, Elijah questioned, "Oh Revealer, what is all this about?"

The voice answered, "Elijah, Elijah just take a closer look and see what is beneath these dresses."

Then suddenly, after a heavy thunder, he saw a lightening flash. At a distance, but in clear view, lo and behold, 251 human beings with all shades of skin colour, fenced in a purple-coloured ring, appeared. A conversation ensued between the darkest of them, Kamara, and the fairest, Uri. Kamara initiated the chat when he saw Uri virtually gawking at him, as if he has not seen an African before.

"What the heck are you looking at me for and what are you doing here?"

"In the first place, I am enjoying the mosaic of different people who seem to have a common goal and destiny with me; and secondly, to express relief that I am not alone in this lifestyle," Uri said.

"After all, as the saying goes, what is good for the goose is also good for the gander," Kamara responded.

"However, I did not think people of your skin colour were this adventurous," Uri answered.

"It depends on what you mean by adventurous," Kamara sought explanation.

"You know what I mean. It did not occur to me that searching for pornographic images on the Internet was your kind of game. You people have always been sportsmen, outdoor people and going directly for the kill." Uri was trying to be specific.

"Oh you mean we do not have what it takes technologically to pave our way into meeting our needs?" Kamara asked.

"Precisely. In addition, I did not think you go for complex and expensive delicacies."

"Where there is the will, a way will be found. Who said these oysters are the preserves of a particular race or skin color," Kamara came in.

"Come on, all activities have levels of expertise. This activity we are talking about comes with expensive gadgets, which I did not think people like you would be able to afford." Uri was becoming more direct.

"Yes, the number of people here who look like you far outnumber my people, but surely you see that some of my people are as advanced as you to be capable of chiselling out the same quality diamond you are after. Furthermore, you have to know that what a man can contribute to the advancement of children cannot be determined by the color of the skin, but by the substance of his life or character, and as you know, the substance of a man's character has never been determined by the color of his skin," Kamara refuting Uri.

"Both of us are vibrating on the same frequency then, if you are saying that our treatment of these children constitutes their advancement as we address their emotional needs."

"What I am saying is, don't look at me like that ever again."

"Kamara, I must accept that I have been naïve and backward in thinking that these adventures are sought only by my people."

"Yes Uri, you have come to your senses early. If you eat, sleep, drink and love kiddies, so do we."

"Hey Kamara, I rest my story and say no more. Let us go for action now." Uri concluded the chat.

"Elijah, Elijah, look at them more carefully," the voice thundered again. Then on their foreheads were written their ages. The youngest was 15 years old and the oldest was 90. The 90-year old man approached the youngest and questioned.

"Son, what on this earth are you doing here."

The younger one became confused, thinking he had seen his grandfather.

"From what I understand, it appears we have been caged for going after the same thing." The young man answered.

The old man muttered to himself, "I did not know that people are starting these things this early." Then he spoke out.

"Kid, out there it has all been about protecting people your age. Who did you get involved with to be here?"

The teenager answered back, "I grew up at the age of 13. You do not have any idea what motivated me to do what you adults are doing."

"Tell me, what have you seen or experienced?"

"My mother's boyfriend who was also my babysitter from the age of nine watched pornographic images with me over a period of four years without my mother's knowledge. I kept it from her. He was my role model and hero. I surely had to practice what he taught me, as I believed he would teach me what was only good. He said all the time that he loved me."

"Ha, you see where we are? Did you understand what he was doing with you? When you get another chance out there, run away from the images as far as possible. Did you put yourself in the shoes of the children your age behind the images? Did the man touch you or ask you to touch him? If our activities were of use, we would not be here. You hear me?"

"I guess so, thank you," the young man responded.

The next thing Elijah realised and became petrified of was the revelation of their nakedness as he was made to gaze at their private parts, after special rays were beamed on their front parts.

He exclaimed, "Oh Revealer, please spare me this."

Protruding perpendicularly out of their very elastic pants, it was clear that 235 of them had active male sexual organs, while 15 of them would not respond to these special rays. They were impotent. The last one seemed to have a very flat front. Further scrutiny revealed the being to be female.

Then as he watched, one of the sexually active men asked an impotent man, "How come your phoenix is still in the ashes but you are having a go at a child for sex. What are you going to put where?"

The impotent man stared at him and said, "your question is legitimate; however, I believe I can raise the phoenix out of the ashes with brand new wires."

The active man continued, "have you seen a plug ever plugged in without pins standing out?"

The exchange was becoming tense. The impotent man retorted, "have you ever seen a big pin plugged into a small hole, and for that matter a square peg in a round hole, you bastard?" Then suddenly, the feuding party heard a deep breath coming from the right side. At close range, they saw the flat-fronted being approaching them.

In a synchronized voice the two men exclaimed, "what on earth are you doing here, woman. If you grab a female child, what will you be looking at since you have the same thing, and if you get hold of a boy, surely not only is his champion incapable of responding to your stimuli, but your tit will be too big for him. You surely have a problem."

She responded, "I am trying to prove that this is a world of equal opportunity. If a man can dabble in kiddie daba doo, so can I. After all, I am a liberated woman and as a bisexual, I have the right to spice my sex life up in whatever way I want." Before they could tell her to find life, the scene faded in Elijah's sight.

That very moment, as Elijah looked on, he saw the 251 beings menacingly moving towards a children's home full of playing children ranging from the age of two months to 15 years. Hope Children's Centre was established to cater for this age group. He heard the voice of a senior woman worker saying to a care worker, "keep your eye on the very tiny ones as well as the older girls and boys. They are all vulnerable. From all angles: their gender, age, disability, displacement through military conflict, refugee status, socio-economic background, peer pressure and low self-esteem issues, it is clear that our children are defenseless people who are easily taken advantage of."

Then the Revealer's voice came on. "Elijah, Elijah, see what they are about to do." And as he watched, he saw them lick their lips seductively and walk to the playground of the Centre. The workers, at this moment, were busy with other things, and had momentarily taken their eyes off the children. Before they were aware, these men and woman had carried as many of their children as possible away. All these beings were carrying under their armpits what looked like laptop computers and webcams. Most of the children were seen coming back, but while some appeared unaffected by their bitter experience, others soon started exhibiting unusual behaviors. They were worse off then before. Furthermore, only a handful could say what actually happened to them.

The voice continued, "Elijah, Elijah, keep looking."

He could not contain his surprise when suddenly, he saw them change into clothes indicative of their religious backgrounds. Elijah opened his mouth in amazement and shouted, "gracious me!" Before his very eyes, he watched as 150 of them worshipped Satan. Wearing fancy masks and in red overalls, they bowed to an image standing tall over a billowing fire. And as the fire occasionally spewed out flames violently, they fell prostrate on the floor a few meters from the fire, repeatedly shouting, "Bubulaja, you are our saviour and we shall obey you to the end of time."

"Yes, go out and be free to do what will give you pleasure. I will keep an eye over you all the time," a voice sounded from the fire.

And as Elijah was being overwhelmed by these activities, the voice spoke to him: "Elijah, Elijah, you will see more despicable scenes, keep watching." His attention was drawn to his left side, and saw 50 of the 251 known perpetrators in church choristers' robes, clapping and singing, "I am a soldier in the army of the Lord, we shall rise again in the Army." Then when the leader took to the pulpit to preach, his first sentence was: "Let the children come to me, for to them belongs innocence."

Elijah, told the Revealer, "I cannot believe my eyes; are these Christians and raping children and watching pornographic images?"

"They only profess with their lips their love for God, but their deeds say something different," the Revealer replied.

When Elijah thought he had seen enough, his attention was drawn to his right hand side. "Elijah, Elijah, what do you see there?" On the heads of 25 of these people were black round hats, similar to what Jews normally wear. And as they stood before a wall and muttered words and nodded their head back and forth, it became clear to Elijah that Jews were also involved in this behaviour. They were practicing Judaism as they prayed. The Rabbi could be heard doing the Sh'ma (the proclamation of faith in a single God) and the Amidah (19 blessings acclaiming the attributes of God), using Hebrew, the language of the Bible. Elijah heard them say, "Grant us peace, for we have sinned." They then praised God and made petitions. This was followed by a procession outside for a public worship led by a cantor who officiated with the traditional chants. Looking at their faces, Elijah could see a sign pointing towards Jerusalem. He was amazed to see little children sitting on the hats shaking with fear and trembling. Will Jews and Internet pedophilia mix?

Suddenly, he heard the sound of the usual early morning Moslem call to prayer. Elijah called on the Revealer, "please don't tell me Moslems are doing the same thing." Turning back, he saw one of the biggest Moscues with a large dome above the main prayer hall. Outside the mosque, there was a minaret from which Elijah could hear the muezzin call Muslims to prayer. Inside the mosque there was a space to store shoes. Then ten men, part of the group, which had just sexually abused children in various ways, washed their ears and feet and entered the mosque and took their places and knelt on floor mats wearing long white robes. They would rise up, mutter some words to themselves and go down again. It was not difficult to discern that they were Moslems. It was clear inside the mosque that there was a Qibla which was facing a sign to Mecca. In this wall, there was a Mihrab, which was a small cove also pointing towards Mecca. Then finally he saw a minbar, a platform where the leader of the service, the Imam gave his sermon. There was no doubt that Moslems are also involved in Internet Pedophilia.

"Elijah, Elijah, just turn your head backwards and watch." The Revealer spoke. He saw five men entering a temple within which were sparkling clean images of heads, hands and legs adorned with a symbol indicative of ash. In a flashback, Elijah saw that just before coming over into the temple, they had finished sexually abusing children on the Internet and seduced some of them into physical contact. They had in their hands something to offer to a god. Just before entering the temple, they took off their foot wear and lay prostrate in front of a flag column facing the North. They then saluted an elephant-headed image. Finally, they were handed over what was purported to be Holy ash as a blessing to be worn and told to say the "shivaya namah". They then offered something to the priest. This was followed by saluting a Goddess and the deities in the temple three times. While in the temple they chanted some five letters. Before coming out they could be seen asking permission to take a token of blessing out. On coming out of the temple, they again prostrated in front of the flag column towards the north. Then it occurred to Elijah that he was observing a Hindu worship. Hindus as Internet pedophiles?

"Elijah, Elijah, let me show you the last of these weeds before you come to yourself. Look up." As he looked, he observed a building with so many statutes of Indian-looking images. And as he looked intensely, he saw six of the men among the 251 enter a building on which is written the word, Gurdwara. It had remained open throughout the day, so that worshippers can offer prayers at any time convenient to them. It was morning to Elijah, and he heard Asa-di-var being sung, followed by the Anand Sahib, the Ardas, a kind of supplication and a Hukam, a reading of the Scripture. This was followed by the distribution of Karah Prasad, consecrated cooked food, made of flour, clarified butter and sugar. Finally, he saw what seemed to be a Guru being ceremoniously wrapped up and taken to a special place for the night.

These were Sikhs worshipping after sexually abusing children! Children were moving around their legs with their hands on their heads and covered with red substances and crying. Just as Elijah realized that Internet pedophilia was independent of religious background, his wife, Bertha, woke him up.

CHAPTER THREE

PROFESSIONALS BEHAVING MADLY

Bertha consoled her husband and both went home. It was about 11:30 pm when they reposed to bed, after making sure that the house was secure. The culprit had not been caught and there was fear that he might strike again, if it was a vengeful act. Bertha was soon fast asleep. And as Elijah sleeplessly pondered over the incident, he found himself in a trance again.

"Elijah, Elijah, let me put you on a mountain and watch what goes on in Metropolisia Cosma."

"Oh Revealer, it is more than I can bear."

"You will be alright," replied the Revealer.

Elijah found himself on the pinnacle of the highest mountain, Mount Onyx, which overlooked Metropolisia Cosma. At this position, the vision was so vivid and clear, and as if looking through a pair of binoculars, Elijah could see the one million people who live on the Island as well as make out the 251 Internet pedophiles distinctly and observe their activities, past and present.

Metropolisia Cosma appeared to be a very vibrant natural harbour city with well-educated workers who were capable of delivering services required of them. With an area of 500sq km and sitting at the foot of Mount Onyx, it looked well protected. The top of the mountain stood at 1500m above sea level. However, it became apparent that Cosma was morally, a city of contrast, and could be termed the "beauty and the beast city". The seedy side was characterized by shanty suburbs, sexual promiscuity, violence, drunkenness and drug abuse. "Elijah, Elijah," the voice called again. "What you saw previously was not as vivid as what you are about to experience. It is daytime now and you will be privileged to see things differently."

In a flash, Elijah realized that the City Island was divided into five zones: the downtown central zone; the south zone, where there are well-besotted beaches; the industrial west zone; the red-light district and shanty east end zone and the newly created residential north zone.

The voice told him, "Elijah, Elijah, for a brief moment you will be a citizen of this community with needs to be met by the city's flamboyant and industrious workers. You will be involved in so many activities enabling you to meet some professionals. Just keep an eye on their respective professions. When you see a child between their legs or on any part of their body or you feel your heart jump or when someone winks at you with his left eye radiating some red rays, understand the signs. That being would be an Internet pedophile. Remember, the emphasis is on their professions."

He suddenly found himself homeless. He was then directed to the central zone to see the Housing Officer for help. A respectable soft-spoken man in a clean-cut black suit came out of a room to meet him with a smile. Surprise, surprise, he had seen this man before, as his heart jumped massively. Elijah, thinking that these people had any recollection of anything in the past asked, "How do you do?"

The reply came, "how do you do?"

Elijah continued, "Do you remember me, Sir?"

"I am not sure we have met before," replied the Housing Officer. It then occurred to Elijah that these people were in a different world altogether. He was given an application form to complete and to send it over to the Property manager responsible for the North Zone, which he duly did.

"Sir, I understand you could be of help to me as I search for a home. I am a new resident in the city."

From the way the manager looked into his eyes, Elijah thought the manager had something against him, which startled him.

"Let me see what stock I have," the manager said.

"Would you prefer a ground floor 3-bedroom flat or a 4-bedroom semi-detached house?"

"The second one, Sir," exclaimed Elijah. It was after the relevant paper work was exchanged and the manager was escorting him out of the office that Elijah saw a dishevelled child pop out of a side cupboard running between the manager's legs and crying.

"Man," he said to himself. "This is surely an abused child."

Previously, Elijah had enquired about obtaining a job. However, he was told to have an address before seeking any employment. After securing accommodation, he was fortunate to be invited for an interview with the Managing Director of an Information Technology Company, METROCIT Ltd. The appointment was at 10 am at the company's headquarters in the West Zone.

Befitting a top information technology manager was a very spacious and well-furnished office.

The first question was: "why do you aspire to this position?"

Elijah replied, "I believe I can help push forward the vision and goals of this company"

"Well answered." He was told. He then winked at Elijah and said, "you are hired." However, the moment their eyes met he felt a special red-hot sensation radiating out of the interviewer's left eye, Elijah new at once who he was. He was successful in his interview and got hired. It was a requirement of the company for all workers to wear a photo ID, which meant him going to the company's photo studio for a passport-sized picture to be taken.

"Gee, you are a beautiful man," the photographer stated.

Elijah thought to himself, "yak, a beautiful man? He must be a faggot." Then as they shook hands, Elijah responded, "I hope I come out fine."

When the camera focused on Elijah, a child appeared in the lens giving him a heart jump and he shook his head. The photographer, not knowing what it was all about cautioned Elijah that he was about to take the picture and that he should steady himself and smile.

It was also required of him to undertake some developmental training course in order to enhance his chances of obtaining a management position. On the training day, he was joined by four other workers in the classroom. They included a computer scientist and three newly-appointment information technology graduates. After they had all taken their seats the Training Manager appeared to give them a lecture. The way he was dressed and held in high esteem by the workers, it needed a third eye to discern the extra-curricula activities the lecturer was involved in. Elijah could not believe his eyes. As the lecture proceeded, there was no doubt that all his companions where Internet pedophiles, as he saw naked children sitting on their laps with their hands tied behind them.

The company's first team meeting involved being introduced to key figures in the company. One by one they appeared in the executive suite: the accountant, business analyst, computer scientists, the systems administrator and the co-opted investment banker. Though Elijah was already in a trance, he was trying to be sure whether he was seeing right. Then it occurred to him what the Revealer told him. "All of them, all of them, double-faced as you see them. Hide your children from them." All these learned professionals were known to him. Then he saw children on the table crying and begging to be freed. "Buggers, they have raped all these children," he told himself. In his trance, he was struggling and wondering when he would come out of his experience. "Elijah, Elijah, you "aint seen nothing yet." "Oh, this time the Revealer is sounding like some one I know." He said to himself. Elijah took a cue from an advice the Investment Banker gave them, which reminded him to go to the bank during the break, which he did. He joined the queue in the bank. When his turn came and he approached the bank clerk, he did not know what was before him until he, Elijah lifted his head. There before him stood a moustached man in a striped blue-white shirt smiling. "How can I help you, Mister?"

"Oh, just to deposit 500 Cosma dollars." His heart jumped, as he saw a bruised and naked boy in his left eye.

The next thing Elijah saw in his vision was his wife, Bertha, beckoning him to come and help her take her things to the house from the Underground train station in the central zone of the City. She came with their 6-year old son, Jojo. Meanwhile, talking to each other behind Bertha were the Underground train driver and the Underground signal engineer. It pertained to signal problems, which caused the train to be stuck underground for about an hour and generated public concern despite the advanced technology in place. Elijah was initially unaware of the two men, until he recognized their voices. He immediately looked forward beyond his wife and recognized these men, who had around their necks children sitting and crying. They also looked at Elijah with a smile, as if they knew him. "Monsters," Elijah muttered to himself.

To get home, they realized that they would need a van, as Bertha brought a lot of stuff from wherever she came from. It took about 15 minutes for the van driver to come after a phone call. Mrs Morrison and Jojo sat at the back, while Elijah engaged in a conversation with the driver, sitting in the front passenger seat. "What is occurring in town of late," Elijah asked the driver. What he said disgusted Elijah so much that if it was not very dark and were miles away from home, he would have stopped the van and gotten out.

"You must be the only stranger in Jerusalem. All of us have abandoned our adult partners. We are revelling in adult sexual interaction with kiddies. Why don't you leave this old woman and try this kid here?" Elijah suddenly saw a child sitting on the driver's lap. He was fuming. Before he could burst out of anger, they arrived at his home. The driver added that he was also a removals driver and would be at Elijah's disposal anytime he needed him.

"What a twisted man that was. He does not have even basic school qualifications. But does that matter? Over my dead body to call you again."

The time in Metropolisia Cosma was suddenly Saturday 06:30. Bertha informed Elijah that she did not have any breakfast items and would need to go shopping. He quickly took her in his car to the best supermarket in the west zone. It was about 06:45 when they arrived at the shop, which operates 24 hours. As he entered the shop, he was met by one of the night stockers, who greeted him.

"Good morning Sir, I hope you have a pleasant shopping session with your lovely wife." At this, Elijah looked sideways and saw a man holding the neck of a crying baby and laughing at the same time.

"Bertha, call the police, this is child abuse." But he was in a trance. The store appeared to be out of stock of Cornflakes and other needed food items. The truth was that they were so engrossed in the earlier experience that they had missed the right aisle. He went quickly to the retail manager of the store who happened to be around who assured him that he believed they had everything they needed in stock and that they should walk over to see the warehouse man. "Could you please help this couple with what they want?" The retail manager told the warehouse man.

"I think we have everything on the floor. They seem to be new here and did not know their way around the store." As they walked with the warehouse man to the right aisle, Elijah looked back at the same time as the retail manager looked back. He winked at Elijah. The kind of radiation absorbed by Elijah caused his heart to jump.

"Then there is no hiding place for our children. How do you protect your children from those who are supposed to provide food for them? God help us." He was thinking aloud. And before he could finish thinking, a child was found under the armpit of the warehouse man with her head facing backward. Bertha could not see anything.

One of the items they bought was an alarm clock. On his way out of the store, Elijah realized that someone had spilled fluid on the floor and a cleaner was on his knees busily mopping the mess. Unfortunately, because Elijah was distracted and looking sideways, he nearly stumbled into the cleaner, who was actually hovering over a six-month old baby girl.

"I am sorry I nearly fell over you," Elijah apologised.

And as the man rose and looked into his face, he felt a big jump in his heart at the sight of the baby.

The cleaner responded, "I am alright."

Elijah told Bertha, "he is not alright, he is as sick as a sickle. They are every where and in every area of human activity. Even this illiterate can use the computer when it comes to Internet sexual abuse of children. Creeps."

Hardly had his thought subsided when he was met by one of the trolley collectors asking him if he could assist him by quickly off-loading his purchases, as business was picking up and more trolleys were needed by new arrivals to the shopping complex. He thanked him and said he was alright. When he turned back he saw him with a child with blood all over her crying in a trolley he was pushing. He felt like throwing up. "Are you alright, love?" Bertha asked.

"Yes, dear, thank you."

Finally, they set off to go home. However, on the way he realized that he did not have enough petrol in his car; hence, he branched to the nearest petrol station to fill the tank. Unfortunately, after filling his tank, the car would not ignite despite several attempts. The car was towed away to the nearest garage, where it was repaired. When he thought it was all over and was expressing his appreciation to the car technician/mechanic, he saw something unusual about him. He was laughing with his mouth wide open. And on his tongue stood a tiny boy who appeared very sad. He then quickly closed his mouth and said, "you are most welcome." Elijah's tummy was churning at this time, and continued so until they arrived at home.

The receipt given them at the supermarket said they could return items, which turn out to be unsuitable or unworkable within 5 days. The alarm clock they bought was set to be tested that very night but would not go off. The following night the alarm clock failed again. Remembering the conditions on the receipt, Elijah returned to the store and straight to the customer service representative.

"Unfortunately, when I bought this clock I did not test it before taking it away. For the past two nights it has failed me, and would appreciate it very much if you could give me a refund or give a replacement."

"Sir, it is clear to me that you have tampered with the clock making it impossible for me to give you a refund. One option left for you is to top the money up and take a better clock."

As Elijah gave him the top up, he looked into customer service representative's eyes and there stood in his left eye a crying baby girl. Elijah felt like slapping the man at the counter.

"Elijah, Elijah.' The Revealer came on the scene.

"I have more scenes to reveal to you. Don't give up yet."

Still in a trance, Bertha asked. "Elijah, when is Jojo starting school, as I am starting work in two weeks, and I understand schools re-open next week? I overheard the other day that there is an excellent school a few blocks down the road."

Replied Elijah, "On Monday let's try the school if they have a vacancy." The head of the school was very pleasant and agreed to accept Jojo the following Monday. On that day, it was customary for the head teacher to introduce parents to relevant people in the school including the child's teacher, nursery nurses for the very young ones, caretakers, garden man, the choirmaster and the scout leader of the local scouts club.

"Elijah, Elijah.' The Revealer called.

"Here, watch those who will wink with their left eye and smile at the same time." Apart from the head teacher, the rest did exactly as the Revealer said.

"Indeed, this is a city of the beauty and the beast. Is there any profession that is exempt from this heinous behaviour?" Elijah wondered as fear filled him for his son.

In the second week, when Jojo went to school with a few bruises after falling down in the family's thorny garden, the school called a social worker to investigate the situation. He went to Elijah's house to make an assessment. And as he questioned the Morrisons, Elijah saw a child with blood over her sitting on the left shoulder of the male social worker with her face covered in dejection and shame.

"You hypocrite child protector. After preying on this child, you are pretending to know better." He was trying to tell the officer, but to no avail as words from Elijah were not heard by these beings. There and then, Elijah decided to move houses, hoping that he would find a better neighbourhood. He did not know what lay ahead of him as foretold by the Revealer.

Before moving homes, the family decided to take a Friday evening out to watch a musical concert and to travel back home. A few minutes into the music festival, there stood before him one of the musicians and the concert pianist, as if to say watch us and our abilities on stage and forget what we do in dark places. Possessing special ability to see through every medium, he could see the audio-visual technician behind the scenes with a baby boy between his legs and trying to pull away from a light string attached to the man's trousers. Elijah felt the whole show nauseating and left the theatre with his family. He had a strong urge to leave whatever country he was in.

The following day as he made an attempt to purchase an air ticket to leave the country, he was met with a smiling face of the travel agent, who was also winking at him with red-hot radiations emanating from his left eye. He had in his hand a child who was dangling as she was held at her left leg. Elijah struggled out of his trance, as he could not believe that the whole professional environment was infested with Internet pedophiles, and as his eyes opened into the real world, he found himself praying: "Oh Revealer, whoever you are, please leave me alone." But it was not going to be the case because the revelations were not yet over. With his senses back, he started wondering whether he was okay. After discussing with Bertha about the frequency with which he has been falling into a trance as well as what he had been seeing, she urged him strongly to see a counsellor. Ruling out any substance misuse or schizophrenic tendencies, he was prescribed some form of anti-psychotic medication, anyway, and admitted for five days to monitor his sleep pattern. The third night he fell into a trance again.

CHAPTER FOUR

BEASTLY NEIGHBORHOOD

Elijah found himself in Metropolisia Cosma again. "Elijah, Elijah." The familiar voice thundered again. "This time keep your eye on the academic qualifications of those who will be involved in your change of neighborhood. You will come to your own conclusion by the end of your move." Prior to moving homes, Elijah had seen a new housing development in Cosma New Town. He enquired whether a special request can be granted for a purpose-built house to be constructed at an additional cost. This entailed having to see a well-known man in the building industry, Bobo, a building contractor by profession, who was well connected to a draughtsman and the foreman at the site. Everything was granted and the five-bedroom detached house was completed in a record time. On the day he was on his way to collect the keys from the salesman, the Revealer's voice came on.

"Elijah, Elijah, open your eyes wider."

"Oh Revealer, I hear you loud and clear." Then as he collected the keys to his new house from the salesman he saw a line up of four men, including the foreman, the building contractor, and the draughtsman. All of them had basic education. After winking at him gladly with their left eyes, they turned back to walk away. Elijah then saw each of them carrying a crying baby on his back in a pouch.

"All these fine professionals prey on children on the Internet to satisfy their sexual depravity?" Elijah questioned.

"But Revealer, which of them caused us this anguish?" Elijah continued.

"You will soon find out." The Revealer replied.

Suddenly, he realized that he had acquired so much property that he needed not only a big removal van, but also a forklift to lift the heavy items into the van.

"Good morning, Mr Morrison, I am sure you will be missed by your old neighbours. Your deeds will precede you." The new removal van driver said, as they carried the lighter items by hand into the van.

"Good morning, Sir, and how much is the going rate today, since you people keep charging new rates everyday," Elijah responded.

"As we have all enjoyed your contribution to this neighbourhood, I guess you will pay only a fraction of the normal. I am doing it for free today."

"Thanks so much, driver." Having been helped by close associates to bring the heavy items near the van, the forklift driver got to business and as Elijah spoke to him, he felt like having a heart attack, prompting him to the sort of man he was. Shortly, he saw a crying 10-year old girl sitting on the neck of the forklift driver and begging to be set free. There was nothing Elijah could do. He was soon on his way to Cosma New Town, the new housing estate, in the removal van. Just after the van was emptied and the driver was about to leave, Elijah saw three children jumping out of his eyes and running in his direction to be taken to safety, telling the number of times he has been involved in this sordid act. Then the van driver and the children vanished. None of the workers he had met so far had a college qualification.

The next move, in Metropolisia Cosma, in the process of moving homes, was to advertise the sale of the old house. Whereas in a normal human world an estate agent is consulted, on this Island, the procedure is different. First a printing company has to be identified to make a big print of the sale poster, which is mounted in front of the house. Then finally, an advertising consultant brings the information into the news media. Having heard of his plans to move, the local electrician, who was also a University qualified electrical/electronic engineer, agreed to disconnect a few gadgets for him. Elijah's burden of selling his house was lifted when he got a buyer. He was a ruthless businessman, who was also known to own a brothel with his pimp brother. He has a postgraduate degree in business administration. Then just after the house was bought, Elijah met with the printer, the advertising consultant, the electrical engineer and the businessman for a drink. His associates on this occasion got so drunk that they started throwing up. To Elijah's surprise they started spewing out children from their mouths. Elijah found himself thinking aloud, "you double-faced brats. Justice will catch up with you soon."

Wedding Ceremony

The date was clearly marked on a wall in Cosma New Town: Sunday 6th December 6666. It was a special occasion for a top civil servant who was known to give a lot of money for good causes in his community. The wedding ceremony became a national issue, which was announced in the local and national Newspapers and on Television and radio. As soon as Elijah heard the voice of the radio presenter, the vision burst on his eyes to recognize the person. The night before the radio announcement, the disk jockey had watched sordid images of children and had masturbated through it. He announced, "in a week's time, we shall witness a momentous event, which will grant our honoured civil servant the licence to live together forever with his beloved wife. We cannot wait to see their offspring, who would also grow to give us amusement!" Elijah was invited and he was so keen to attend.

Before the wedding, Elijah received an invitation from the Office of the Ministry where the civil servant worked. It was an express mail delivered personally by the postman. He knocked on the door and when Elijah came out he said. "You need to sign this paper to confirm delivery of this important post, please." Elijah signed the paper. It was when the postman was saying the word, "thank you" and his mouth opened widely that Elijah saw a 6-month old baby wearing a nappy stuck in his throat crying for help. He was horrified. "But if these people are not exposed the way I am seeing it, how could we know them?" Then when he went to the newsagent in the corner shop to buy stamps to post his reply letter confirming his intention to attend the wedding, he was met with a smiling face at the counter. The popular newsagent has always been with his wife in the corner shop. To Elijah's consternation, the newspaper the man was reading had a live picture of a child on the front page, with tears flowing from the child's eyes. The man winked at him with his left eye after giving him the stamp. "What on earth is going on here, even people with little education?" Elijah exclaimed.

To keep abreast with the latest fashion for men, Elijah visited a men's fashion designer, who specialized in wedding suits.

"Can I be of assistance to you, Sir?" The designer asked.

"Of course, you can. Can you please measure my size and give me the latest for the civil servant's wedding ceremony?"

"Take a look at our brochure and make a choice."

Elijah did as he was told and was given the following day to come back for the suit. On arrival, he picked the brochure once again to compare the actual suit with what was contained in the brochure. They matched perfectly. And as he and the designer were discussing how the picture matched with his actual design, he saw children jumping out of the designer's office with outstretched hand seeking help. He had already paid for the suit for the fast track sewing so he could not leave the suit behind. However, he could not wear it for the occasion. He bought another one somewhere else.

On his way home he remembered that his best shoes were not in good shape, as he had worn the same for many years. This time he felt he should buy a new pair. Nevertheless, he was not going to throw the old pair away, since it was only the soles, which were a bit worn out. He was happy when the nearest shoe repairer, who was just a few meters away, was pointed out to him. Having bought a new pair of shoes, he went to see the shoe repairer. It was a "wait while we fix it" shop. It did not take long for the repairer to bring the pair back. The moment Elijah's hand touched that of the repairer during exchange of money, he had a massive heart jump, as he saw a baby boy jump out of one of the shoes crying, and when Elijah gave the man a second look, he winked at him with a piercing left eye to confirm his fears. What he was witnessing was very appalling, but he was determined to participate actively in the wedding and he wanted to go there well dressed. He felt out of fashion wearing the same cufflinks and seeing his wife always in the same necklace and earrings. This prompted him to look for the best jeweller in town. Where else could he find the best jeweller, but in the industrial zone. Hence, off he went. This is a jeweller, who, he was told, had a very attractive and serviceable wife and one would not think for a second that his eyes would ever be diverted to another object of sexual desire. Having no children between them, there were rumours, however, that his wife could be barren. The man was known to have an illegitimate son. Elijah bought the jewellery he needed for himself and his wife. It so happened that, at the same time as he gave Elijah the boxes of jewellery, he licked his lips and as his tongue pulled out Elijah saw a dishevelled child sitting on his tongue and crying for help.

Being Catholic, the civil servant's big day was to be officiated by a prominent Catholic priest. The Revealer spoke. "Elijah, Elijah, watch the unfolding scenes carefully as the blind leads the blind." In his pontifical dress the priest waited at the usual place in front of the congregation. The whole ceremony was so well-planned that the moment the priest came to the fore, the wedding march was initiated and a special "may they live for ever thereafter" song was sung by a 100-strong choir. The bride and the bridegroom made their way to their seats in front. The exchange of vows followed.

"Would you Dollarcent take Poundpenny to be your wedded wife for better and for worse until death do you part?" The moment Dollarcent, the civil servant, said, "Yes, I do," a child in the congregation gave a distressing cry. There was a short pause, as both the priest and Dollarcent looked in the direction of the cry. The final step was when the priest had to give the bridegroom the Holy Communion. The moment he gave Dollarcent the bread, the bread changed into two children jumping and limping. One went in the direction of the priest and the other went towards Dollarcent. They were both naked boys. "Elijah, Elijah, have you understood what is happening?"

The wedding party was held in the Central Hall of the City's only University, Cosma University. It was attended by various prominent people, including University students, researchers, catering staff to cook and voluntary workers to serve. Elijah was also there. At the sight of these participants he felt a sensation in his heart, as he absorbed radiations from all corners of the hall, indicating that at every corner a horde of predators lie in wait for children. Innocent and decent as they appeared to the public, prior to this event they had all abused children on the Internet and some of them had had physical sexual encounter with the children. On the dancing floor were these children beating their abusers and asking to be set free. Only Elijah could see the children.

Just as the party was about to end, the journalist/photographer, in his tuxedo, asked Elijah if he would want to pose for a picture.

"It will appear in Cosma News," the photographer said.

Elijah replied, "why not."

As the camera was focused on him and he snapped, Elijah saw a naked child running out of a flashing lens. He quickly identified the photographer as one of the 251 people he had met earlier in this saga.

Military Action

Then suddenly Elijah observed that the political scene in Cosma had changed with frequent rumours of war between Metropolsia Cosma and the Xylocon Tribe, who live on another Island. The population in Xyclocon was about three million. The Xyclocon Tribe were pugnacious, but were not developed much in terms of advanced war techniques. They relied more on their numbers. For the past 50 years this Tribe has been a thorn in the flesh of Cosma. Consequently, Cosma has never stopped arming herself and getting her military power up-to-date. On 12th December 6666, Xyclocon threatened to attack Cosma again. Cosma has always been at the cutting edge of war technology. The Chief of Staff summoned his top military officers to the Peace Suite of the military headquarters for briefing to find every means to avoid an all-out war. This was to be achieved by flying fast planes over enemy territory and dropping flyers to warn them of the implications of a continuing threat. Elijah, somehow found himself in the Suite. Around this big oval table were the chiefs of the Navy, Air Force, the Army and Special Forces. Behind them were top-notch regular military officers, both men and women. As Elijah followed the proceedings, his eyes got glued to three men: a naval officer, an army officer and an air force pilot, all decorated and with advanced University education. Their positions behind the table indicated that they were highly respected men. But on their decorated medals sat three sad children with outstretched hands asking to be rescued. These top military officers were picked to lead their units on the assault on Xyclocon, after they continued to taunt and threaten Cosma.

"But if these officers cannot control their basic instincts, how are they battle-ready to defend a nation?" Elijah questioned himself.

"Elijah, Elijah, let me tell you once again that you have not been sufficiently disappointed and shocked," the revealer thundered.

The war went on for seven days until 19th December 6666, after which though Metropolisia Cosma won, they sustained serious setbacks, including the death of ten of their soldiers. Many other officers suffered major injuries.

Hardly, had the war problems subsided when a terrorist activity ripped apart one of the buildings of the Embassy of an allied country. No one died but ten people sustained fatal injuries, and were flown by helicopter to various hospitals. As Elijah looked on, two police officers were assigned to the scene, a uniformed one and a plainclothed one, who was an established communications officer in the police force. It horrified Elijah that people into whose hands public protection has been entrusted could set themselves against the law they are supposed to enforce. It was revealed to Elijah that these police officers would relieve their work and family stresses by masturbating as they dabbled in pornographic images of children on the Internet.

Two of the most seriously injured men ended up in the top military hospital in the city, where they were attended to by top Consultant Surgeons, nurses, clinical social workers and counsellors, all well-respected professionals with University degrees. Meanwhile, the blood samples of the injured people were given to the hospital's top biomedical scientists for analysis. "Elijah, Elijah, take a closer look at these professionals. You would think your children are safe in their care. Think again. Tell me what you would do with them. They have all abused children on the Internet."

"Oh Revealer, you are the only one to tell me what needed to be done to them."

"It will not be long, and you will know their end."

A few of the injured men sustained both mental and physical disability, which necessitated them being put in care homes in the eastern zone. Even in this zone, where one would think that the poor and needy would keep to themselves, it came to Elijah with shock when he suffered a massive heart jump, after setting his eyes on some people with learning disability and in receipt of disability living allowance and also pensioners. They were sitting down quietly and looking innocent. But that was not the whole story. They whiled away their time abusing children on the Internet, whenever there was no one around.

"The whole world is on a roller coaster to feed on the innocence and vulnerability of children." Elijah thought to himself.

Other professionals in this sector of the city were also involved. Once a while, mental health nurses, legal advisors, benefit officers and opticians came to the eastern zone to visit the feeble and the needy to meet their needs. The person who coordinated the activities relating to care homes was a nice-looking male clerical assistant. Elijah was there on this occasion and was waiting in the waiting room when coincidentally, all the aforementioned professionals met to be cleared by the clerical assistant before going to the main complex to discharge their duties. As they vanished into various rooms, Elijah saw children in different emotional states following each of these professionals. Elijah shook his head. On his way out of the compound, Elijah turned to wave the clerical assistant goodbye. His hand was barely up to give the sign of goodbye when he was given a big wink from his radiating left eye. He hurried out of the area. A child was pointing an accusing finger at him. As he struggled to come out of his extended sleep, he found himself in a large forest strolling. He was met in the park by a man who introduced himself as the park ranger, who asked whether Elijah was lost. Elijah replied, "I was rather wondering whether you were lost. What are you doing here with this crying 5-year old girl?"

"Elijah, Elijah, what have you learned so far?"

"Oh, Revealer, you have revealed to me that Internet pedophilia is independent of education and profession. But please, let me alone. Enough is enough."

"Do you want to see the one who caused you this anguish?" The Revealer questioned.

Elijah, by this time had been in the hospital for four days and on this occasion, he was found to have slept too much. He was forced to wake up when Bertha visited. He woke up startled and gasping for breath and muttering," you murderers and rapists, you will be weeded out." The neurologist who was standing by assured Bertha that everything would be fine.

CHAPTER FIVE

TOPSY-TURVY RELATIONSHIPS

After exchanging pleasantries with Bertha, she left around 11:30 pm for home. Elijah then took his medication. He was looking up to the ceiling with his eyes wide open and suddenly he fell into a trance again.

"Elijah, Elijah, I am fully aware that you have been wondering whether there was something wrong with their relationships causing them to go after children." Suddenly, Elijah found himself in a big office and on the wall behind his chair and table were the words "Elijah, Chief Family Counsellor", and sitting before him were 250 men.

"Why did you want to see me, all of you?" He asked them.

"We have heard of your practice and wanted to chat with you about some things going on in our lives of late."

As Elijah was given special powers to scan their brains, even before the words came out of their mouths, he could make their thoughts out and made mental notes of them, taking particular note of the narrations given by twenty of them.

The audience cited separation, divorce, difficulty in relationship, dead partners as reason for the offences; some also cited being single, inability to form lasting relationships; others gave vivid incidents of childhood abuse, including bullying and behavioral problems causing them to opt for children; yet others cited additionally that their parents were either separated or unsupportive of them; a few of them were adamant that their relationship was intact when they were involved in the offence of Internet pedophilia. Most of them cited more than one set of factors. These are sample statements he told Bertha later, and the challenging questions he posed them.

"You know what, Elijah, I had an unhappy childhood. The relationship between me and my brother had for a long time, prior to this lifestyle, ended acrimoniously due to dispute about money. I was previously married and had a 15-year old daughter. My marriage ended after I had a stroke and my wife was not willing to look after me. I then started chatting on the Internet, while in some kind of platonic relationship with another woman. Since my current conviction, my parents and only sister have ceased to contact me."

"I understand how awful you might have felt in your sense of loneliness sometime ago. But what made you think you would obtain any form of happiness by relating with children on the Internet?" Elijah countered.

"Having become fairly immobile and bored, I thought such an activity would engage my mind and libido."

"Considering the consequences of your behaviour, how would you rate your success in the venture overall?" Elijah questioned.

"Elijah, it is obvious that my thinking has been wrong."

Another one spoke up. "Elijah, I had a caring and loving upbringing. My mother was virtually over-protective and did everything for me. Then I started having relationships with women to the extent that I stopped relating with my parents in any meaningful way. My first relationship was a married woman, which lasted seven years. Then, impotence set in causing me to lose my family, though there were occasional erections. With time, the impotence became pronounced and my relationships became of short duration. Then I gave up completely relating with women and turned to the Internet for kick starts. I got hooked for 5 years."

"You might have sought consent from the women in your previous relationships, and I believe they were well informed. My question is: was it possible for you to seek approval from the children who were supposed to kick-start your sexual activity? If so how, if not why?"

"Surely, I could not seek any particular kid's consent because I was just making use of images."

"How do you think your daughter would feel if she was the image being used by many men for their sexual gratification, and for that matter, do you sincerely believe that you were justified to use the images you are referring to?"

"Well, some of my friends were doing the same thing, so why couldn't I?

"You said your parents were over-protective and doing everything for you. Are you saying that they were so protective that you lost your ability to make your own decisions? If so, would you say that despite knowing that what your friends were doing was wrong, you could not decide to do otherwise?"

A different man spoke up. "Elijah, listen carefully to my story. My childhood was confusing. I do not know the identity of my father, neither have I been close to my mother. I was brought up by my grandparents who had 18 children, including my mother. My mother was of a similar age to some of my uncles and aunts. My mother remarried and had three sons with this chap. But Elijah, I did not count in this house. I was forced to live with my step-father because my grandparents could not control me. But it was worse with my step-father, and I returned to my granny's house. I married and even had three children with her. We had good sex. However, I became a drunk and would come home and beat her up, until we split and the children were taken into care, after that my wife went mental. I finally turned my attention to children on the Internet for sexual gratification."

"You were indeed messed up in your childhood. But what were you trying to achieve by turning to alcohol?"

"The thought of my previous experiences were too bitter for me, causing me to blank them out with alcohol."

"Considering the recurrence of drunkenness and where you find yourself at the moment, would you say that turning to alcohol was helpful?"

"I would not say it helped me, but temporarily I felt I was managing life and empowering me to venture into Internet activities."

"If you thought relating sexually with children on the Internet was the answer to your problem, why did you not approach it legally or in a socially accepted manner?"

"But Elijah, that was not possible."

"Then are you agreeing with me that the way you went about it was illegal and that you knew what you were doing was wrong?"

Another person approached him. "You know what, Elijah, I was deeply involved in Internet pedophilia for a long time until I was caught. I lost two wives due to this behaviour. Though I had two daughters with my second wife, I was hooked on this behaviour until she could take it no more. We were having sex alright, but the feeling of squeezing something out of my penis whilst watching these kids in different poses got the better of me. I must be a monster."

"What makes you think you have been a monster?"

"Right from the beginning I knew what I was doing was wrong as my conscience pricked me incessantly, but I ignored it. Only a beast behaves like that."

"It is good you have come to this conclusion yourself. It indicates you are prepared to do whatever you can to stop the behaviour. Do not look back."

"Counsellor, following the breakdown of my relationship, I went to live with my mother. I was deeply upset and experienced suicidal feelings and feelings of depression and isolation. Working in loneliness as a minicab driver, I started spending more time on the

Internet for adult porno and then veered into kiddie ones. I liked to look at "attractive children in various stages of undress".

"Yes, having no one to talk to can put someone on the verge of insanity. But can you explain to me how your involvement in Internet paedophilia could overturn your feelings at the time?"

"I was having uncontrollable sexual feelings after my relationship broke down. Hence, I turned to pornographic images to help me picture what I was doing with my wife, if that would give me some relief."

"Did you think of the consequences of such a behavior?"

"I thought in my privacy, everything was fine and I should be allowed to do my own thing."

"What evidence did you have to prove that your suicidal tendencies and feelings of depression would be alleviated by viewing pornographic images of children?"

"The euphoria I had in masturbating through the images was proof enough, what do you think."

"In view of the fact that normally married couples in a sexual relationship do not end up in prison, do you realize that there could be something wrong with the way you went about meeting your sexual needs?"

"What can I say about this, Elijah?"

"Elijah, I have been single all my life. I had an unhappy adolescence, which was made worse by my parents" separation resulting from my mother's infidelity. My siblings and I were regularly exposed to domestic violence. Then my father was unfairly asked to move out of the house. Later on I resented and rejected any affection expressed by my mother, whom I initially held in high esteem, and grew closer to my father. Consequently, I could not form any lasting relationship with women. I became reliant on Internet child pornography to express myself sexually. I could not trust any adult woman, who to me, may behave like my mother."

"I can see that your trust was betrayed by your parents. But how were you going to regain this trust by getting involved in Internet pedophilia?"

"I was not thinking of regaining any trust, but it occurred to me that impersonal as Internet pornography may be, my sexual needs would be met without actually interacting with any human being."

"I am confused here. Did you think about the origin of the images of the children you were using?"

"What do you mean, Elijah."

"What I mean is, your trust was betrayed by your parents and you became disturbed. What do you think would become of the trust of the children who were lured into making those pictures?"

"You mean those children's trust was also betrayed? It has never occurred to me."

"Not only that. Have you thought of the fact that not only were their trust betrayed, but by not seeking their consent in the production of those images, they were virtually raped, and you are still participating in their rape?"

"Elijah, I may continue my single life. I have never seen my real father. He died when I was 3 years old. I lived with my step-father, who would sometimes, for the slightest mistake, use either his fist or belt to beat me when I was younger. At 11 years, my friend's mother touched my penis. My older step-brother also sexually abused me. At 17, my apprentice boss took me fishing and when we were alone, he made me suck his penis until he was about to masturbate. I have tried to relate with women but they never lasted. I am a confused man. In isolation and loneliness, I found sexual satisfaction watching naked children on the Internet."

"Yes, your situation can be confusing and put you off relating with adult women. But I have this question for you. Do you think you have related with enough women, statistically, to conclude that no woman on earth can give a lasting relationship?"

"But Elijah, I cannot try all women to come to that conclusion."

"Then what makes you think images of naked children on the Internet can help you in achieving a lasting relationship?"

"Elijah, whereas with images of children I can always go and have my sexual feelings satisfied, with real human beings, as the relationship breaks down so do I have a break in meeting my needs."

"Think about it. Are you not implying that you think about yourself alone and how your needs would be met, and that you are hiding behind the Internet selfishly?"

"Counsellor, I hope you will understand and help me. My father was never present in my life. He suffered from schizophrenia for a long time. I grew up with my mother and younger brother. I found my older brother too arrogant. My mother suffered from regular bouts of depression and was always taking anti-depressants, which affected me. I always felt for her. I have never had any intimate sexual relationship with an adult, because I get nervous when I had to touch someone. I kept all these to myself. I remember when I was 14 years old some older women forced themselves upon me for sexual encounters. I did not understand much what they were doing with me. Later on in life, I felt older people would mess up with my life. Hence, I started seeking sexual satisfaction by looking at images of children on the Internet during my quiet times."

"I know the experience you had at 14 affected you immensely. But what do you think children who are being used to make these images feel?"

"Elijah, but I am not touching children physically."

"Do you see the link between the experience you underwent and got messed up and the experience children in the images experienced before you got the images?"

"Are you saying, Elijah, that I am somehow condoning the abuse of children?"

"Yes, imagine if the women had not only forced themselves upon you, but had also taken pictures of what they did and someone was watching your images for sexual satisfaction. How would you feel? Of course, your perpetual abuse."

"Elijah, I am gay, but I have been afraid to come out. I am always confused about which gender it is better to relate with, a man or woman. This has prevented me from having intimate sexual relationships. I think this was due to severe physical abuse I suffered from my father during childhood. My parents have always treated my like a child, and I have become forever emotionally attached to them for approval on virtually everything. But I get erection and the only place I found solace was looking at pornographic images of children and relieving myself sexually."

"You have raised so many issues, and I can understand your confusion over who you really are in terms of your sexuality. However, how did you plan to remove this confusion through involvement in Internet pornography?"

"I was thinking that momentarily, anonymously looking at both female and male naked images and feeling good sexually would not cause me to relate with a man or a woman until I am sure of myself."

"And what makes you think images of children would serve your purpose best at this time, as against perhaps controlling yourself until the right time?"

"Elijah, controlling myself was out of the question, but I was of the opinion that such images are for anybody's use."

"As the images are that of actual human beings, did you think of how the dignity of the children behind these images would be affected?"

"Elijah, my father died when I was 12 years old. I never got over this and became depressed. Somehow, I became so withdrawn that I never became motivated to relate with any female adult. I am not sure about my mother's involvement in the death. Gaining knowledge about the Internet helped me to use it to meet my sexual fantasies."

I am sorry to hear of your father's death at a tender age. You might have loved your father dearly. But you did not indicate even trying to relate with your contemporary females to see the result. Did you form a negative opinion of adult women at your father's death?"

"No, Elijah. Since I did not have any experience relating with women, I was afraid it would not go well with me."

"What concrete evidence did you have to conclude that it would not go well with you and adult females of your age, and therefore children would be the best solution to your fears?"

"I did not have any basis except my gut feelings told me that. I was able to lure this girl off the Internet for sex because she readily responded to my show of affection without the hesitation of an adult woman."

"Would you then agree with me that you preyed on her innocence and vulnerability, as she was not well-informed?"

"In your heart of heart, and considering where you find yourself now, do you really think your actions were in the best interest of the child?"

"Elijah, do you have any idea what belittling is? My father and mother separated when I was 7 years old. I then lived with Dad. It has been a nightmare, as if I caused his marriage to break down. Most of the time, he told me I was not going to amount to anything. In effect he made me aware that I would not be successful in whatever I did. I lost my virginity at 15 with a 16 year old girl; at 17 years I had another sexual encounter with a 13 year old girl; at 20 I had sex with a 20 year old woman. Then at 28 I had a four- year relationship with a woman. The last one was a difficult relationship, which eventually came to an end. Since then, I found solace on the Internet watching child porno."

"I appreciate your instability in relationships for whatever reasons. But how was finding solace in watching child porno going to stabilize you?"

"Somehow I formed the opinion that being bored with the private parts of adult females, that of children would give me a change of scene, which would reduce my ongoing stress."

"In your estimation, what was the probability that the images you watched were obtained with the consent of the children involved. And if it was without consent, what would that constitute?"

"Elijah, I am not able to respond, but I know that sexual relationship without consent is rape."

"Would you then agree with me that most probably, children were being raped for your enjoyment, and if so you perpetuate the rape of these children?"

"Counsellor, I am now 30 years old. I had a happy and stable childhood until my parents divorced at 11 years. Before this separation, they were arguing most of the time in Spanish, which I did not understand. They were so much into themselves in argument that they did not have time for me. My mother had a mental breakdown later. I realize that I harboured anger and resentment toward the couple for not being there for me. I felt guilty for possibly being the reason for the marriage breakdown. Eventually, I married but I was also involved in Internet pedophilia as a past time. I was not getting full sexual satisfaction from my wife. Then after I was caught, my wife's stepfather committed suicide by taking an overdose of heroin."

"It is sad to realize that it all ended tragically. Nevertheless, can you tell me more about your inability to enjoy full sexual satisfaction."

"It would appear she always wanted to end the sessions before I wanted to, indicating that she was not fully involved. In my mind, she was not, as usual, there for me."

"What made you think naked images of children on the Internet would complement your unfulfilled sexual encounter with your wife?"

"Elijah, you should not ask me this question. Being not fulfilled, I would, of course, be engrossed wildly in kiddie porno to masturbate until I feel complete."

"Why did you engage children and not adults in your activities?"

"Elijah, I am sorry to say that though they excited me, I did not consider exposed children's private parts as of any significance."

"Are you saying you did not have respect and regard for the dignity of children?"

"Sort of."

"Then reflect on where you are now and think again."

"Elijah, I had a disruptive childhood after being abused sexually by my stepfather. I was taken into care. I never knew my real father. In my sexual promiscuity, I made a girl pregnant and had a son who has always been with his mother. I am keen to make contact at the appropriate time. I do not think I know what true love is, since I never experienced it. I get sexual relief now from looking at pornographic images of children."

"I understand where you are coming from, and I sympathize with your seeming lack of real love and consequent loss of direction in life. But in watching pornographic images of children on the Internet, how do you suppose you will know what love is?"

"I was not intending on obtaining love from it, but knowing that I may not obtain any love from an adult female in a sexual relationship, I am comforting myself at the expense of kiddie images where I know I would not experience rejection in my quest for sexual satisfaction."

"You did not tell me how many women have rejected you so far, so on what basis do you conclude that any woman you will relate with will surely give you a cold shoulder?"

"Elijah, I simply fear that my expectations are not going to be met, so I have not made an effort to date a woman since leaving my son's mother."

"So what value do you place on children to make you think that your use of their naked images would meet your expectation?"

"I have not thought of the real children behind the images and what they feel; all I know is that there are some things about them that are portrayed that can meet my sexual needs for as long as I have not found a loving adult female."

"If your life was messed up because of lack of love, do you think the children were being loved when their images were being made available to you and others. If not, don't you think you are playing a part in messing their lives too?"

"Counsellor, I feel it is a norm to abuse children. All my life I have always been sexually and physically abused.

My stepfather physically abused me. Two men sexually abused me and at 15 a man sexually abused me. I am just trying to see how abusing a child looks like. I watched child porno and then got a 13-year old girl and sexually abused her. Good score, eh?"

"It is sad to note that you have been through a number of abuses. It appears you realize now that all that happened to you were wrong. So how does your wrong-doing added to what was done to you make life better for children?"

"Seeking revenge is all that motivated me to do this."

"You feel you scored well for what you did. Then do you agree that you deserve to be where you find yourself presently, since you believe in an eye for an eye, which will cause all of us to be eventually blind?"

"Elijah, at 11 years, I was asked by an older man to masturbate him in a public toilet, which I enjoyed for helping someone. Then it became my lifestyle to sexually relate with older men throughout my teenage years. Then with time, I adopted a lifestyle of occasionally having sex with males I met at Gay clubs until I became impotent. My philosophy was that since I was attracted to older men when I was a child, it was my turn to be attracted to children as an older man. I love them and their lovely small things."

"You said your enjoyed what you did to the older man. What makes you think children will enjoy manipulating your genitals?"

"The man convinced me that males sometimes play with their parts, so I always used the same techniques."

"Looking back, did you think you had enough knowledge about such actions to consent to his plans?"

"Nope."

"Well said. Then don't you think you were forcing yourself on the boys you met, as like you, they did not understand what you were asking of them to do?"

"I did not consider forcing myself on them."

"Considering your situation presently, and reflecting on your intention to pass on your experience, do you think your past experience has worked in your best interest? If not, do you think, overall, your scheme would have served society any favour?

"Are you listening to me, Elijah? I had a good relationship with my wife. She was disabled after a second whip-lash injury. We mutually agreed that whilst she uses a vibrator in her bum, I also watch my child porno to do my own thing. We became sexually satisfied and then went to bed. Is this wrong, Elijah? Sexual intercourse with each other was a pain and inconvenience. Where else did you think I should seek sexual joy?"

"I am sorry your wife went through such trouble. But what exactly is watching child porno to do one's own thing?"

"You have to understand, Elijah, that I could not control my sexual urges."

"But what is the evidence that under your circumstances, the only way to satisfy your sexual urges is to watch pornographic images of children on the Internet?"

"I did not gather any evidence. It was all over the news that people were deriving some satisfaction from the behaviour, though some of them were being caught, but I decided to take my chances."

"Have all the chances and risks you have taken in life ended up where you are right now? If not what does it tell you about society's attitude towards your behaviour?"

"Counsellor Elijah, I and my wife were in a relationship for thirteen years and it has been wonderful. My wife did not interfere with my extra-marital computer games. Though, I did it secretly, she was very supportive of me in my involvement in the criminal justice system. I was enjoying sex with her and topping it up with this new adventure."

"What kind of sympathy do you think you deserve?"

"I believe in a democratic society, I deserve to be allowed to please myself."

"Do some others have the democratic right to take pictures of your naked daughter or son and use it the way you did?"

"Maybe."

"Do you think they would have any respect for your child?

"I do not care."

"You have to start caring, because children have rights, which you are abusing, and where you find yourself now indicates that society will vehemently resist your machinations and that of others of like mind."

"Elijah, Elijah, the voice sounded. "What did I tell you?" "The nature of relationships does not matter. Now have a look inside a courtroom".

"This is indeed men behaving madly." Elijah replied.

Just before the trance ended, a shadowy figure came past Elijah. He could not see his face but he saw clearly the letters AN on his back.

CHAPTER SIX

COSMA CROWN COURT

In the Crown Court of Metropolisia Cosma, the Judge walked in.

"Rise," the court usher announced. The High Court Judge took her seat at the high table. Below the Judge sat the court clerk, liaising between the barristers representing the Internet pedophiles, and the public prosecution officer, representing the government.

"Elijah, Elijah, open your eyes and follow the court proceedings. Your dream will soon come to an end," the Revealer thundered.

It was a special court with a very big room, including a dock capable of accommodating about 300 offenders at one time. The public gallery was also huge. This special occasion was sentencing day for these Internet pedophiles. As Elijah scrutinized the faces of the defendants, it suddenly occurred to him that he had encountered all of them earlier, as their faces were familiar.

"How could these nice people be brought together as criminals? Surely, one cannot judge another from outward appearances."

"Elijah, Elijah, you used to be disgusted with them abusing children. Listen to what they deserve and why."

"Your Lordship, the prosecution will state the factors underlying the presence of these people today. These I hope will convince you that these men and woman standing before you today are all guilty and evil."

"The first factor is the rationale for and the extent of distribution of images. I also need to inform you that there were elements of commercial gain involved that is likely to aggravate the offences and increase their seriousness. Likewise, there is evidence of massive distribution of obscene images, which should be considered a commercial enterprise, even if it did not involve financial gain, since such activities increased demand for images."

"The second factor was the nature of the material. Based on practice procedures, ten classifications of images have been produced ranging from non-sexualized pictures through explicit erotic images to actual sexual assaults, including sadistic bestiality. This range indicates ascending order of seriousness. A related factor was the form of the material in question. As you saw earlier, there were moving images, which should be regarded as more serious than if the same were still images. I will not classify video recordings as such, which is regarded as a compilation of still photographs, rather than a record of abusive activity that has been filmed."

"The other consideration is the age range, the number of children and whether the children involved were of one or both sexes. Recent images appearing in court indicate that there is an increasing demand for pornographic images of younger and younger children of late. It is noted that the abuse and exploitation of very young children, including babies causes much public revulsion, whilst older children, including young teenagers are exposed to psychological damage. Seriousness also depends on the level of exploitation or the nature of the conduct to which the children were subjected or in which they were depicted in the images."

"The fourth factor is the quantity of material possessed and distributed. I know that what constitutes "small" or "large" can be debatable. However, Your Lordship, the consensus is that there should be a balance between the number and the nature of the images. I am convinced that possessing or distributing even a small quantity of material depicting serious exploitation may be more serious than offences involving a larger quantity of less explicit images. Thus quantity may not be the most critical factor to affect the determination of seriousness. However, it should be considered together with the nature of the material and extent of any distribution."

"My Lord, these offenders' involvement with the original offence is also paramount. This audience will agree with me that taking an original image of the sexual activity and transmitting it through the Internet is more serious than just downloading an image from the Internet. I am therefore convinced that downloading for personal use should always be taken as simple possession. In the case of a perpetrator who shows or distributes indecent images, a more serious view will be taken if there is evidence that the offender in some way encouraged or was directly involved in its production."

"The sixth factor is the offender's character. Are any of these here today of previous good character? Surely, some of them are. It is felt that if this were the case, then the conviction would have a salutary effect on him and reduce the seriousness of the offence. However, I dispute this and can state that a person of good public standing may have the seriousness of his offence aggravated by his position in society, since there might be an element of betrayal of trust."

The High Court Judge then took his turn. "May I ask the Barrister for the offenders before us today, if he has any mitigating factors to present."

"Yes, Your Lordship, the effect of conviction, especially resulting in a custodial sentence, will be influenced by the seriousness of the offence. But surely you are aware of how they may be affected by way of losing their means of livelihood, loss of reputation, attracting social stigma, being moved to a new locality now or in future and loss of family. The final point to state is the age and maturity of some of my clients. A number of my clients are simply very young, immature and psychologically unbalanced. Hence, a less serious view must be taken of the offence. Your Lordship, your attention must be drawn to these factors."

"Prosecutor, do you have any counterargument before sentence is passed?"

"Yes, Your Lordship, the latter factors stated by my honorable friend cannot hold water. They are neither mitigating nor aggravating factors. With regard to even guilty pleas, I have taken into consideration the timing and circumstances of their behavior. They cannot be given full credit because they all had little choice but to plead guilty because they were caught with their pants down."

Passing Sentence

"Would the defendants rise, as sentence is passed," it was announced.

"The Court, considering advice from the jury has formed the opinion that the seriousness of your indecent images will be determined based on five levels of activity: I am classifying your images and seriousness of your behaviour according to whether they depicted erotic images without any sexual activity; or

if they portrayed sexual activities between children or masturbation by a child; or if they involved non-penetrative sexual activity between adults and children; or whether they depict penetrative sexual activity between children and adults; or if sadism and bestiality were involved."

"Additional aggravating factors I have considered are an impression that the images were portrayed on the computer in such a way to indicate a more or less sophisticated approach to trading or a higher level of personal interest; or if the images were posted on a public area of the Internet or distributed in a way that made it more likely to be found by computer users who would not intentionally be looking for pornographic images; or, if in addition to you being the originator of the material, you also used your own families, those from particularly vulnerable groups and/or those over whom you were placed in a position of trust."

"Depending on these guidelines, and listening to your barrister, I am dividing you into fiver groups. Group A1 of ten defendants, group A2 of fifty defendants, group A3 of sixty defendants, group B of one hundred and twenty six men and group C of five offenders. Group C, made up of five of you will be made subject to unpaid work or conditional discharges and fines because you were only in possession of material solely for your own use, including the fact that the material was downloaded from the Internet but not further distributed, and consisted entirely of pseudo-images. The material you made did not involve abuse or exploitation of children, and there was no more than a small quantity of material at level 1. I am imposing conditional discharge on some of you because, in addition to pleading guilty, you had no previous convictions."

"I am imposing community sentences on those of you in group B because you were in possession of a large amount of material at level 1 and a small number of images at level 2, and the material was not distributed or shown to others."

"For those of you in group A3, you passed the threshold of a custodial sentence because it is proven that the material you possessed was distributed to others, and a large quantity of material at level 2 was found and a small amount at level 3 also. Some of you in the group distributed or exchanged indecent images at level 1 and 2 on a limited scale without financial gain. Hence, I imposed only up to 6 months in prison."

"For those of you in group A2 who distributed a large number of images at level 2 or 3, and also possessed a small number of images at level 4 or 5, I am imposing between 6 to 12 months in custody. And for those whose possession involved a large quantity of material at levels 4 or 5, even without distribution; or who distributed a large number of materials at level 3 or traded in level 1-3 materials, you are being made subject to 12 to 36 months custodial sentence."

"Those of you in group A1 will receive sentences from 36 months to 120 months, as you were found to have distributed images at level 4 or 5; you were also actively involved in production of these images at level 4 or 5; there was breach of trust and you committed the offence with intent for commercial gain. In addition, you were found to have initiated and facilitated the production of such images and/or had previous convictions for involvement in child pornography, sexual abuse of children and you were violent to children."

"Before I ask the guards to take you away to serve your sentences, does any one have anything to say?"

To Elijah's surprise, a man by name Delta and another man, by name Pi, raised their hands.

"Yes, Delta, what do you have to say?"

Delta looked sideways first, and looking straight into the Judge's eyes said that, "I am sure some of your sorts are doing exactly what you say I have done. You will all go to hell. I do not deserve 120 months. I must be free because the laws you are citing against me are not universal. If I was in a more civilized country, I would have been free. My actions are not morally wrong. The laws in this country are clearly flawed. On top, how can I obey national laws when I am dominated by superior laws given by witchcraft power?"

Delta then made an attempt to jump out of the dock. But before anything, he was held down by two guards and led away. The Judge then said, "if I had my own way all of you would be in prison for life, but I gave you some credit, as elaborated by you barrister.

"Yes, Pi, what is it?" He pointed his raised middle finger at the Prosecutor and said, "have you forgotten that when I met the girl she pretended to be 17, when in fact, and without my knowledge, she was 12 years. She sent me a photograph of someone older. She led me on. When we met at the local shopping centre, she was dressed like a prostitute. Where then did I go wrong? Also, my desire for sexual contact is very strong, which is not my fault. I cannot control myself. Probation should have treated me the last time they had me."

"Take him away," said the Judge. Banging the table with his wooden gong, she signalled the end of the Court session. Just after the last offender vanished in Elijah's sight the same shadowy figure he saw as a family counsellor followed. On his back was written ANAC, and he vanished. Elijah shook his head in disbelief.

"Oh, Revealer, what do you say about the fairness in the sentencing?" Elijah asked.

The Revealer explained. "Examination of the sentencing guidelines as explained in the cases discussed above, points the way to a wide range of issues about decision-making by a Judge. She was trying to interpret and apply the law; but comparing her expected responsibilities with what happened in practice portrayed a different picture. All sorts of factors and variables influenced the process. The legal standards are the central point of focus, but she had to use a lot of discretion in order to be seen to effect control measures. Clearly the Judge's decision was based on her perception of seriousness."

"Now faced with this array of factors, it would appear that she would be bound to do a lot of hard thinking on some of the circumstances surrounding the offence in order to decide on the sentencing option. The extent of discretion and objectivity would invariably affect severity of punishment. Given a set of standardized factors, a judge would have to determine the extent of deviation from the factors and come to conclusion whether the offence, on the whole is serious or not."

"There is a lot of debate going on about the effectiveness of imprisonment. However, it is borne from experience that, in the short term, custody serves as a deterrent and protects the public and sometimes the defendant from harm. The longer the sentence, the more the public feels justice is being done and the offender becomes aware that his offence was serious, causing him to reflect on his behavior and change his attitude to the offence. In the criminal justice system of Metropolisia Cosma, the extent to which an offender is motivated to refrain from re-offending and maintaining that stance in practice determines the success of preventative measures."

"What I am trying to say, Elijah, is that it is possible for a judge to come to a conclusion in his sentencing option, which would not reflect the true seriousness of an offence and hence affect the extent to which his goal of reducing recidivism is achieved. As explained above, these discretionary factors eventually affect the extent of justice meted out and hence the effectiveness of preventative measures."

"However, what the Judge did was in line with the fact that Metropolisia Cosma has the right and duty with regard to maintaining order among its citizens, and that lack of such duty would cause civic disorder and alienation. "Knowledge of and respect for civic order is an overwhelming ethical and practical political necessity, which serves to prevent social unrest and revolt. However, in a constantly changing world, it is clear that at no time can it be said that all tactics employed by perpetrators have been known and therefore there is no need to consider any further changes in the law."

"Thank you very much, Revealer, for your explanation."

Public Reaction Outside The Court During Sentencing

There was a lot of media attention on the sentencing when it was in progress. Hence, outside the Court, there was a large gathering. Many of them held placards, others wore special T-shirts and others had loud speakers to voice their concerns and express their opinion. Many messages were posted in various ways. They included, "You dare not mete out community penalties like Conditional Discharges and Unpaid Work. With such a penalty, their distorted thinking would not be challenged."

One person commented that, 'you do not allow a bankrupt to work in a bank, so why allow a pedophile to work in a school.'

"Our children have been abused. Give us access to discovered pornographic images and so that we can delete them. The images of our children may still continue to be abused by pedophiles."

"Name and shame them," one loudspeaker was mooting.

On a T-shirt was written, "How can a pedophile be released from prison to return to the same home from where he abused children?"

Elijah then saw a Police Officer explaining something to a placard holder. "One of the most important decisions is where sex offenders will live. Unfortunately, there is no home, which is far from a school or shop. The needs of the victims are taken into consideration, along with a lot of other factors connected with the prevention of future offending. Sometimes those assessments have resulted in a sex offender returning to an area where his victims live, on the basis that he will be known. It may be close to a supportive doctor, to family or to people who would be able to spot signs that the person may be about to re-offend. Do you understand?"

A bystander responded, "this is unbelievable."

A mother said, "I have five children of my own and we have a baby in foster care with us. How can the Judge let any man of such nature live between us and a school, which has 100 children? This is beyond my understanding."

On another placard is written, "you have to ask what on earth is going on here when a man who is supposed to be in prison for abusing a child, and had previously been convicted of assault on boys, can return to the community and no questions asked. Doesn't the Judge understand that he will re-offend and ruin the life of another child?"

A placard had these words: "there should be a new offence of grooming, which will give the police the power of arrest before any sexual activity occurred, and there should be a civil order to be brought against adults logging on to chat rooms and pretending to be teenagers."

Two months later, an Internet child sex offender killed himself after he was forced out of his home by a mob of screaming youths. On the estate where he lived, there was no sympathetic reaction to his suicide. However, his grieving family rallied against the media for creating a climate of hysteria over Internet pedophiles, which led to the abuser's death. The Internet pedophile took medication for heart problems after suffering a stroke, as he could not face the world anymore because of the hysteria surrounding this type of crime. He then swallowed 150 tablets at a time and died. In addition, many perpetrators were reported to have become so worried and depressed because of their involvement in Internet pedophilia that they developed more serious diseases or have made attempts to commit suicide.

Not only did the public react towards the phenomenon itself, but in various ways, they also reacted towards some of the rulings made by the Courts. Some of the reactions have been positive, though. The debate has been about how society should balance the right of the individual who has been convicted of such a crime and has served his sentence against the right of the victim.

A man voicing his concerns on a loudspeaker said, "let them receive the maximum penalty, even if it means life for life. Even burglary cases can attract many years. We are disappointed that despite child abuse being always a serious issue, lenient sentences could sometimes be given, sending out contrary message to child sex offenders."

A placard just in front of the Courthouse read, "please police, let resources to tackle Internet crime of this sort reflect sentencing. We want to see indeterminate sentencing. Lock up dangerous pedophiles without any evidence before they strike again."

Another placard said, "vet teachers, including foreign teachers and people in positions of trust before allowing them to interact with children."

In Defense of Public Reaction

"Elijah, Elijah, do you know the reasons for these reactions?" The Revealer questioned.

"Oh, Revealer you alone can tell me."

"Elijah, Elijah, I am giving you a sixth sense of understanding."

Then as Elijah looked on, a slow-moving screen with words inscribed on it appeared, and as it scrolled down slowly, he started reading:

"Not only has child abuse in general and Internet pornography in particular had effect on children. The phenomenon has also had an effect on the general public, especially the parents of the children directly affected. This has been expressed in various ways, including the formation of vigilante groups, public outcry and general hostilities, as you saw."

"The question is whether public outcry is justified and why the normal majority of people fear the phenomenon. Elijah, this phenomenon is quite different, which elicits hatred towards the perpetrators. Hostility towards a set of people whose behaviors differ from one's own is an almost universal human nature. Preconceived opinion against pedophilic activities is a perfect example. Its very existence challenges fundamental assumptions about how children should be protected against corruption and exploitation."

"Elijah, pedophilia has never been without reaction from concerned members of society. A culture of animosity against such behavior has been identified since the phenomenon became widespread in recent decades. Some factors may be cited, which may be significant in influencing such reactions. One such factor is prejudice, which refers to an intense, irrational fear of, in this instance, pedophilia on the Internet; a pathological over-reaction presumably caused by internal mental conflict. Such a conflict can occur when a person, with his own definition of sanity is unable to contain insane pedophilic tendencies. He feels children are threatened by these subjectively unacceptable impulses which, invariably, results in violence against the pedophile. The hostility demonstrates intolerance towards or dislike for Internet pedophilia, even in an era of honest liberalization within society, and greater tolerance towards all forms of sexual orientation. It is evident that if society did not protest, the likelihood of government intervention would be far less."

"There are yet other factors that give rise to the continuing dislike of Internet pedophilia and why the responses are hostile. This is because these criminals have been perceived to be child abusers and traitors with warped thinking, a psychological or emotional condition characteristic of a minority of people and not mainstream society. It is these ideas which have resulted in the creation of a sense of responsibility on the part of the law and a defensive attitude on the side of the public. What is emerging is a sense of responsibility to censor and punish a category of people with anti-social behavior. This role is acting in much the same way as some criminal laws. Just as some criminals are treated or punished in order to keep the rest of society on the alert to protect its future, so is this reaction. In this way, society is made aware of the boundaries between acceptable and unacceptable behavior, with a view to control and restrict some patterns of behavior. Elijah, at the heart of the issue seems to be societal protection. Are you with me?"

"The arguments in respect of control and prohibition of child pornography on the Internet will also depend on one's perception of danger, which can be real to some members of the community. There is the danger that society's judgment would be harmed. This is reflected in such hostility that intends to ward off Internet pedophilia because it publicly portrays an obscenity. The implication for child pornography on the Internet is that, arguably, the use of children to produce pornographic images and the possession and distribution of such photographs are activities which are capable of corrupting and exploiting children, as well as having the potential of the perpetrator's behavior resulting in actually sexually assaulting a child. Generally, it would appear that public reaction is borne from the perception that harm is done to children through Internet pedophilia and that the protests you witnessed were justified. Society has the impression that only in the defense of public interest can state intervention (public reaction) or coercion be justified, and that such public reaction must be pitched against actions that threaten the every existence of children's rights."

"Elijah, other broad reasons for hostility and criminalization can be advanced. These include the notion of offence, whereby public reaction is thought necessary to prevent hurt or offence in the sense of insult to children; or the sense of morality, whereby a behavior of this sort is deemed inherently immoral and thus must be prevented, irrespective of whether or not it harms or offends children."

"Another insight can be given why there is intense public reaction to pedophilic activities. This originates from the present perception of the existence of a line between childhood innocence or purity and adulthood perversion.

"Let me give you some history, Elijah, a long time ago, children and adults were essentially treated the same. However, over a period of time when new educational knowledge and practices increased, a moral separation of children from adults was recognized. A new perception of childhood was formed, as children were thought of as clearly innocent beings who needed protection from corruption, which characterizes the lives of adults. The child must be given special protection before being considered mature enough to join adulthood, and this would be accomplished by family, church, school and other social institutions. The protection went hand in hand with control over the child's life by restricting his liberty. Though, the idea of childhood transiting into adulthood had always gradually evolved, and with this transformation imbued with the godly notion of innocence, it is the concept of moral innocence of the child that has caused the opprobrium over the abuse of an age group considered incapable of committing crimes, and who are being exposed to sexual activities prematurely."

"Elijah, consider the term "doli incapax", criminal justice attitude to childhood innocence. It is a further support for the difference between a child and an adult. The original idea is that infants between 8 and 14 years of age are presumed not to be capable of knowingly committing crimes. But this presumption may be rebutted by evidence of mischievous indiscretion by a child, or intentionally doing wrong. However, it is public knowledge that many children of this age group do get involved in serious criminal activities, which is not expected of them. The criminal justice system responds by categorizing offenders by age. This clearly is an attempt to create awareness of the special need to protect childhood innocence. Hence, members of the public become "shocked" or "appalled" that some children committed crimes not expected of their age. The term often used then is delinquency: a child straying from childhood; a young offender, who has ceased to be a real child and needs special treatment."

"Another characteristic of childhood, apart from purity and innocence, is its association with childhood sexual inactivity and adult heightened libido. In other words, it is expected that childhood and sexual activity must be mutually exclusive and be regarded a taboo, sacred enough to guard against such pedophiles, and if it is infringed upon, for the reaction to be quick and hostile, and intolerable punishments that no situation would merit must be seen to be meted out to these people."

Elijah, presently, there is a great challenge to sexual relations between children and adults. Adults tend to exercise control over the sexuality of children because they expect them to be sexually inactive and to remain as innocent beings who need protection and hence impose all sorts of conditions on them to maintain their perception of childhood. It is being suggested that just as a bridging arose due to the notion of new forms of inter-gender communication and the dissolution of previous forms of male-dominated sexuality, a situation that may have caused rampant male violence against women, there also exists a reduction in intergenerational gap due to the transformation of adult-child relationship resulting in sexual violence against children."

"In addition, on several occasions, for various reasons including political maneuvering, book accounts, reports on sexual abuse of children, and recurrent moral and legal crusades against permissiveness and pornography, unnecessary anxieties are generated that increase the likelihood of damaging and counter-productive over-reactions to few sexual incidents involving children. In other words, the interaction between media hard sell and public zealousness and fear about changing human aggressiveness feeds into massive outcries against any form of abuse of childhood sexuality.

"Elijah, from what you have seen so far, do you subscribe to the opinion that the bottom line of indecency of sexual offences against children may be an issue of power struggle, domination of the stronger and advantaged and licensed abuse of trust, which are thought to be the bedrock of violence against children, and that society must fight against this potential violence?"

"What I know, Oh Revealer, is that children undergo painful and fearful experience against their wishes instead of warm and affectionate relationship, and it is this that causes the public to react."

"Well said, Elijah. If your daughter had not been murdered after the sexual abuse, have you considered what she would probably be going through after the rape and the pornographic imaging? Let me tell you, there is every indication that sexual abuse during childhood can play a role in the development of subsequent problems, ranging from anorexia nervosa to prostitution. There is also every indication that for most children, who have been subjected to any form of sexual abuse, the image of the abuse is permanently imprinted on the mind of the child concerned. What did you observe about the children who were carried away from the Hope Children's Centre?"

"Psychological and emotional consequences could be identified, both in the short-term and in the long-term. Initial effects include reactions of fear, anxiety, depression, anger, hostility and inappropriate sexual behavior. Others include low self-esteem, lack of confidence, self-hate, feeling as an outcast, unworthiness, unloved and feeling degraded, guilt, difficulties in school, eating disorder, running away from home and prostitution. In the long-term, victims may lose trust in others and yet through an immense need for nurture, affection and support enter into a series of other relationships that are equally abusive and exploitative. They may feel helpless and hopeless, accepting their fate as inevitable, with resignation and apathy, and have little regard to a future in which they see more of the same abuse. Some use drugs to lessen the pain and blank the perception of reality. Others have poor concentration and loss of ability to structure and use time. They feel powerless and unable to effect change in themselves. Many have retained or adopted societal views of themselves as immoral and corrupting and to be blamed for their situation. They survive in an atmosphere of violence and intimidation where their very lives depend on compliance with their continued exploitation and abuse. Adults who were abused when children are now more likely to manifest depression, self-destructive behavior, anxiety, feelings of isolation and stigma, low self-worth, a tendency towards re-victimization and substance abuse. Difficulty in trusting others and sexual dysfunction, impaired sexual self-esteem and avoidance of or abstention from sexual activity are other characteristics."

"The suggestion is that involvement in child pornography has been among the most difficult experiences for children and juveniles to cope with. These children experience long-term humiliation, with feelings of dirtiness pervading all images of themselves. The problems become compounded over time, partly out of inability to disclose the exploitation or to resolve it in any healthy manner. As juveniles and adults, they have an overwhelming sense of being out of control in their lives, even despite long and intensive supportive care. The situation is described as being one of psychological paralysis arising from extended and repeated phenomenon that leads to habitual helplessness."

"Elijah, let us recap what you saw and read. So what, in a nutshell, can possibly cause the public to react to such phenomenon and, in so doing, call upon relevant institutions to put in place measures to control the behavior? Are you ready to make any contribution?"

"Yes. I can gather from the explanation you have given that Internet pedophilia is a threat to the young. You categorized the threat into two distinct forms: the need for a degree of protection from corrupting influences. As children participate in making these pornographic images or are exposed to them on computer screens or in print, they assume that there is nothing wrong with engaging in sexual activities. The other view is the idea of encroaching upon the innocence of a child. Growing up as corrupted and/or abused children, there is a tendency for them to form the opinion that they can treat other children in the same way they were treated when they were young, thus perpetuating this illicit behavior." Elijah answered.

"In addition, there is the fear that the image of a child in a sexually explicit position could be identified and be seen by many people over a long period of time. This would be shamefully unbearable for the family. This situation gives cause for persons charged with the regulation of such activities to exercise control to prevent the fear of harm and to protect the public. No one knows whether many children who have been missing for a long time, were won over through the Internet and may have been raped and killed. This has affected not only families but also whole nations."

The Revealer continued. "In one form or other all the experiences stated earlier could constitute some form of danger to the State. Such danger poses risks to the very fabric of society itself. The main reason is that families make a state. Any effort to destroy members of a family is an attack on the state, especially through this particular phenomenon, of which many families do not have much control."

"Furthermore, with the possibility of pedophiles grooming their preys on the Internet and eventually physically assaulting them sexually, and in view of some perpetrators having homosexual tendencies, the various images of homosexuals being unmanly, cross-dresser, often swinging both ways, yet also often married stirs up fear in the public. This is because not only does eventual physical sexual abuse of a young boy or girl in a family cause emotional and psychological damage to the child and his family, but the traditional view of the homosexual as a threat to the normal pattern of social conduct and family life comes to the forefront. The boy victim may be exposed to homosexual behavior and internalize it as worthy of emulation. In addition, since there is a common perception that some homosexuals are not best suited to positions of confidentiality, trust, seniority and responsibility, because they are made vulnerable to the issue of betrayal, then the fear is that another set of homosexuals (young male victims) is being nurtured through pedophilia, who would be a threat to the State in future; namely, a danger to national security. Do you see the point, Elijah?"

"If there are sections of the community whose sexual preference is for very young people, and can ultimately sexually abuse them, then there should be considerable disquiet about the impact of Internet pedophilia on some vulnerable members of the community; namely, children. This implies that the prevailing traditional notions of homosexuality as deriving from deviance or evil and increasingly moving along the lines of sickness and mental illness can apply to pedophilia on the Internet. In addition, society's link between such behavior and the incidence of sexually transmitted diseases such as syphilis and gonorrhea would elicit hostile attitude towards perpetrators of child pornography on the Internet. Whilst these diseases are both now less common and more easily controlled and treated, pedophiles with all sorts of sexual orientation face the much greater threat of being labeled as the carriers of AIDS, Acquired Immune-Deficiency Syndrome. The previous notion of AIDS being mainly transmitted within the gay community still persists in some minds. This perception is another example of the popular folklore and homophobic propaganda of some members of the community, though the incidence of AIDS-related illness is now known to be a problem for both homosexual and heterosexual communities. Nevertheless, another disturbing connection between pedophilia, within the context of homosexuality and threat to health, has been established and internalized. In this regard, girls are seen to be in greater danger."

"Public reaction has been used as a means to call on the government to put measures in place to control the sexual abuse of children on the Internet. Making public the effect of the phenomenon both on the victims and the perpetrators has been part of the scheme. People have reacted because of homophobia, fear of harm to their children and threat to civil order. The effects on children have ranged from anorexia nervosa to inappropriate sexual behavior. There is a general fear that the young, the family, the state and the health of the future generation are on the path to destruction."

"Elijah, the above discussion has highlighted the problems faced by children who are abused. If the public did not know this, or they did not do anything about it, by way of protestation, do you think justice would have been done? Parents see their children being damaged physically and emotionally, and as a result have collectively created awareness in the powers that be to act on behalf of the victims. There have been occasions when public reaction has resulted in some families of perpetrators being harassed and even some perpetrators taking their lives, but this does not compare with the advantage of public reaction advancing the cause of regulation of Internet pedophilia. Consequently, more resources have been put in the effort to confront this phenomenon. Not only that, but pedophiles have become aware that their activities are under scrutiny, thereby, frustrating their efforts to some degree.

Finally, the basic premise that children have a fundamental right to their dignity and to freedom from exploitation and abuse would be established and maintained. Children are empowered thus through responsible members of the community."

CHAPTER SEVEN

GLIB TALK

All the custody cases were initially held in one prison, the dispersal prison unit, before being processed into various prisons around Metropolisia Cosma. As they argued about the different lengths given them and cursed the Judges that it was all unfair, they also bragged about other reasons they got involved in Internet pedophilia, whenever the opportunity presented itself.

Elijah, as usual was privileged to find himself among them, acting as a prison officer. What he heard nearly made him mad.

"So what benefit did you derive from what you did?" He asked one of those who got five years.

"Looking at it carefully, I wonder whether I derived any benefits at all. I guess I was motivated by greed," he answered.

"What do you mean by being greedy?" Prison Officer Elijah counter-questioned. "You have to understand what I am saying. Besides my partner, I was having an affair with another woman. That was not enough. I also became hooked to child pornography, viewing the nakedness of small girls and through it masturbated for more frills. I was never sexually satisfied."

It was dinner time. All the prisoners gathered in the dining hall. On one table, an old jailbird, a well-known arsonist, questioned one of the newly arrived prisoners.

"Hey, you, can I ask you a question?"

"Why not," the answer came.

"Rumours have it that you were an Internet child abuser. It was not my fault I became an arsonist, but a child abuser must be a demon. What caused you to do that?"

"What? I have not even seen you before. Where did you hear this from? I will cut your tongue out if you don't tell me. Anyway, you too, what brought you, like myself, into this dungeon?"

"Answer my question first, you devil." The arsonist replied.

"It is shameful, but I somehow found myself in a state of self-centredness and excessive desire for kiddie sex and power. Everybody seemed to abuse me one way or the other. Maybe I should have been a bit more assertive. I had the impression that older people must abuse children. Then my turn came, I thought, when I lured this 12-year old into a bed and breakfast. And as I abused her and set a webcam on us, I felt very powerful. I thought it was normal. I regret now, but then it was simply fun."

"Yak, you do not deserve to live. This is worse than my crime of arson. Get out of my sight."

It was about 10:30am the following day. A few prisoners were left in the showers, including one of the Internet pedophiles who just arrived. He could sense that somebody was behind him as the water gushed on him and then felt that something was brushing against his bottom. He turned suddenly only to come face to face with a naked man with mutilated nose and one eye.

"Don't fear. I have been watching you since you came, and I think you are a nice guy, despite abusing children. I would have killed you myself if I did not think well of you."

"Look, step aside because I am not gay, and leave me alone."

"Faggot, you mean? Don't annoy me. I am here on a peace mission. You want to know what happened to me, if my face scares you."

"What happened to you, whoever did this to you?"

"The geezer slashed my face with a crowbar, and I killed him. Kid, what brought you here?"

Stunned, he said, "not to worry. It's one of those things."

"One of what?"

"She lived a few streets away. She was a 15 years old girl who looked like a 17 year-old. She spurned whatever love I gave her. I swore that I would seek revenge in whatever form. I lured her into my house and spiked her drink. It was pure revenge and sexual gratification under camera, hoping that, thereafter, she would be drawn to me. I eventually ended here."

It was dark. The Internet pedophile shared the same cell with an obviously religious fanatic, a river worshipper. He was a cocaine smuggler across a river over a period of ten years. He attributed his success to the river gods. He also seemed to be on the brink of madness, as he mostly spoke about river ghosts, who urged him on. On their first night together, he asked the pedophile, "what on earth were you doing with the children, son of Satan?"

"I do not regret what I did. I proved myself a genius. I sort of had the Adam and Eve syndrome."

"What are you talking about?"

"It came to a point in time when I was reading too much about Internet pedophilia and how children suffered under it. I also observed the reaction of the public, and I thought to myself, "let me experience first hand what really happens to these kids. My curiosity was further fired when I read somewhere that child abuse is a taboo, a sacred cow and forbidden. I guess I wanted to taste a forbidden fruit. I then set my eyes on my best friend's 10-year old sister, as I went to his house often and trustingly, I gave an impression that I could manage her alone, if need be. My opportunity came one day. I showed her some pornographic images and encouraged her that if she did the same thing, I would give her anything she wanted. Forbidden fruit is what has brought me here. I betrayed her trust completely."

"You imp, it could have been my sister. Get out of this cell quickly into hell."

Suddenly, Elijah found a man in front of him. On his forehead is written his name, Coe.

"What were you thinking, when you abused that child, Coe?"

"I have always thought I was a smart kid and could do great things with the computer. I eventually graduated as a computer scientist. Pursuing my ambition to master complex systems, I wanted to create pseudo-images of naked children. I became hooked as they looked very real. My close associates loved them, as I passed them on. It was pure fun using the computer at will. It was intellectually challenging and satisfying. Now I am reduced to rubbles.'

It was in the prison library. Two newly arrived prisoners met and started on the Judge who sentenced them. The older one started: "what they said about me was all lies. This is the truth. I had been impotent for sometime due to too much drinking. I then detected some activity in my champion when I reduced my drinking for sometime. The activity increased each time I watched pornographic images of children, not adults, as recommended by a friend. I would then masturbate for sexual gratification. Then I thought I could gain full recovery if I physically did it. I managed to get this 12-year daughter of a bitch into my room, but before I could start any thing, the police pounced on me. The saddest part was that my champion did not reactivate."

"Poor you. My case is different. My intention was to fight the law which said child pornography was illegal. I would snort cocaine, stay all night and watch these images. The modern Western woman was too complex for me to get her to bed. Secondly, who is it to tell me what is good or bad for me. This is my lifestyle. So, mindless of the law, I downloaded and did my own thing. That was to indulge in Internet pedophilia as a means to validate and justify my pedophilic behaviour. I was convincing myself that the behaviour or obsession was normal and it is shared by thousands of other sensitive, intelligent and caring people. Why should the Metropolisian government interfere in my affair?"

Church Service in Cosma High Security

"Elijah, Elijah, you are now a priest to speak to these four lads in Cosma High Security prison. After service, Elijah, invite those who want to talk privately with you." The Revealer spoke to him.

"All those who want to have a chat with me after this service can see me in my office. May God bless you all and have a pleasant Sunday."

As he made his way to his office, he heard a voice behind him, saying, "wait Rev, I need to confess something to you. Your message hit me really hard."

"Sit down and speak on, my son."

"I was unemployed, but through illegal activities like burglary, I managed to buy many kids-friendly electronic gadgets. I was inviting so many of them to my house for gigs and games. We sometimes hand-wrestled. Then I would intentionally let my hand slip in the direction of their private parts, whether girls or boys and pretend I did not know what was happening. Occasionally, I showed them pornographic pictures of other children having sex and we shall make fun of that. Then one day this boy came in alone. He said he wanted to see the picture I showed them the last time. I guess I seduced him and encouraged him to freely participate in oral sex. I used the images to show him what he should do. Because my friends relied on me for original images, I took several pictures of him, lying to him that these pictures would be used for "sex education" and that he had made a good contribution to society. Rev, I tick when I look at kiddie images, so I also keep these pornographic images to ensure that there will always be an image of a child at the age of my sexual preference, which for me is between 9 years and 13 years. I then threatened him that I would show the pictures to his parents, friends and others, if he spoke to anyone about what we did. My goal was to keep him quiet for ever. Obviously, it did not happen like that. Rev, pray for me."

"May your faith in the power of prayer keep you looking up to Jesus, the Savior."

Immediately the first man left, he heard a knock on his door. "Son, what brings you here? Can I be of any help to you?"

"Yes Rev, I have a network of friends, who do not hide anything from me. I also try to treat them the same way. Of course some of them are pedophiles, and I exchanged pornographic images with them as a means of establishing and maintaining trust and friendship with them and as proof of our shared intentions when establishing contact with other like-minded people in public and private sex markets. Rev, I then had easy access to other sex markets and to other children. I found the whole experience profitable, in the sense that a market was set up to sell child pornography images, whereby I made home-made compact disks of pornographic images and sold on one-to-one basis. You know, sometimes we needed to have a break or holiday. We then sold our self-produced materials to finance trips overseas on visits and to popular sex tourists' destinations. Rev, I need your prayers to end this behaviour."

"I am happy you have taken the first step of acknowledging that what you did was wrong. You have become aware that you betrayed the dignity, respect and interest of children. When you get out find work to do and associate with people who are making positive contribution to society and never look back."

"Rev, I have always felt inadequate since adolescence. Does my face indicate a man who cannot perform? Each time I had dated adult women, they doubted whether, I had what it took to make them happy. My masculinity has always been challenged. I have been unfortunate not to have adult partners. Hence, I have been inclined towards children since I discovered the potentials of my libido."

"My son, I understand your feelings, but children do not understand what you do to them, neither are they able to consent to what you do to them. What does that tell you?"

"Rev, pray for my soul, for I have been raping them."

Elijah was at the door coming out to go home when the last church member asked for an audience.

"My son, you nearly missed me. Feel at home and tell me what is on your heart."

"Before I came to prison, I was an entertainer and a musician. It was a high profile and stressful position, if you know what I mean. I had to work several hours per day to fulfil my commitments. By the time I come home either my wife would be asleep or I would be tired. I would keep awake until past 2 am each night. You do not need any stretch of imagination to guess what would relieve the stress and get me to sleep. The issue served the purpose of providing temporary escape from negative or unpleasant situations. And with the constant and immediate access to the Internet, pedophilic images and masturbation served as convenient escape mechanism for me during times of stress and loneliness."

"Son, your body is the temple of God, and you have to keep it pure. Go and sin no more."

In the Gym of Metro Central Prison

His chest was very broad, muscular and hairy. He was fortunate to end up in a prison, which was well-equipped with sporting gadgets. He was in the gym all the time to do weight lifting under supervision.

"Beta, your work-out is going very well. You could have prepared for the Olympic Games. What did you think you would achieve by this behavior. I mean Internet pedophilia?"

"Boss, have you joined any elite social club before? If so, do you recollect the requirements of this club? I was in that situation. I was driven by the prestige and pride of joining an elite sex club, Sexa. We met either physically or on the Internet through video conferencing to set relevant agenda. One main goal was to provide a certain number of new horrendous pornographic images per year. Consequently, before I was caught, I virtually abused all the children of members of my immediate relatives to achieve the yearly requirements of a specific number of indecent images. In my case one thousand five hundred new images. I was the club's president, and that means being a leader in the provision of the most gruesome images."

"Yes, Beta, I am a member of an exclusive social club, but I did not maintain my membership at the expense of anybody, especially children. They are the future leaders of every nation. If we mess them up today, we shall have leaders with serious psychological problems. Do you understand me? I hope you have taken a cue by being involved in the criminal justice system."

Plink was a great swimmer, and having a break in the swimming pool of Metro Central Prison. Resting after swimming up and down the pool a couple of times, he was joined by another swimmer. "Have you thought of escaping from this hell one way or another?" Plink asked his companion, a bank robber.

"Knowing what you did, I wouldn't recommend adding you to my list of prisoners who may need to escape. Were you mad in abusing those children? Bank robbing is questionable, but taking the innocence of a child deserves going straight into hellfire. What was your motive, son of perdition?" The friend replied.

"You think your crime was better than mine, eh? You have left so many people in financial ruin, just as I have left children in ruin. But I will tell you what moved me, hoping that you tell me your story? Plink answered.

"Go on then."

"For me it was a matter of supply and demand. The market was there, the financial incentive was huge and I took advantage of it. I became a guru in the supply chain. My informants made me aware of the fact that customers were becoming bored with watching the same images all the time, and that they wanted new pictures, which could be pseudo-images or involve real children. Hence, to meet their demands, I had no choice but to partake in this behavior that would not have existed if there were no desire to obtain some benefit. Sometimes I bought tickets for sex tourists to go wherever the kids were known to be financially and emotionally unstable to lure them with what would make them feel better in order to bring me live pictures, which I passed on. Lucrative, I tell you, but the coppers were not asleep."

"Pity, son, very very sad story. Next time I will take you to the Hope Children's Centre where they keep children severely damaged by you."

Theta, an Internet pedophile and another criminal, a wife beater, were locked in isolation in different rooms for separate in-prison offences. The rooms were divided by a thin wall, through which the faintest noise could be heard on the other side. They then got talking.

"Theta, you are a nice-looking man, who could have any woman you wanted. How come you went for a kid? You frighten me over my own children."

"Yes, you wife beater, I had a wife and a 6-year old son that I may not see for a long time. I am an amateur art collector. Upon hearing about this phenomenon, I thought I could keep some of these images for the future, when I could make a lot of money if I sold them later. A pedophile friend taught me the art of identifying a series of images, and to make big money from dealers, the images must be supplied in a particular order. Some pedophiles may be missing some of the series and may seek through the Internet for someone who has the missing parts, and that is when I came in. I was well-known in the underworld."

"And the only means to achieve your greedy lifestyle was to prey on children? I hope that when you die, the world would come to an end, because if it does not and everybody takes up your lifestyle for survival, all our children would be severely damaged."

Open Air in Polisia Detention Centre

Polisia Detention Centre was an open prison for those whose sentence was about to come to an end, or whose level of risk and seriousness of offence was deemed low. Two Internet pedophiles, Bruto and Phanta ended there. A few months before being released, they were assessed for preparedness to be back into the community.

Elijah, who was sent to be a release assessor, asked Bruto why he committed the offence and whether he had become aware of the consequences of his behavior.

"Sir, I thought wrongly that only a child was capable of sexually arousing me. Adult females of my age group never moved my champion. Children became my preferred sexual partners because at the sight of children I was turned on sexually. It appears unusual but my champion would go into top gear at the sight of naked children at playgrounds or in pornographic images. Somehow, I could relate emotionally with a child in a way which was quite different from that with adults. There was some agreement or correspondence between my emotional needs and that of children. Another reason was that I could come down to their emotional level and was able to respond to their emotional needs. I was always after very vulnerable children who needed my attention and comfort. I was indeed living in the world of Peter Pan, never wanting to grow. I believe I am now an adult who should set his priorities and standards high. I am ready to go out and do this no more."

"On one hand you indicate a person who has a heart for children; on the other hand, what pours out of your heart was always contrary to their interest. How do you reconcile the two?" Elijah asked.

"Assessor, I was screwed up. All my records in this prison will tell you that my head is now on," he spoke apologetically.

"We are going to keep and eye on you when you come out." Elijah warned him.

When it was the turn of Phanta, he answered thus.

"Sir, I regret my behavior profoundly, and with what I have learned here, I believe I will not disappoint you if you let me out. Let me explain. When I was younger, around fifteen years of age, I underwent some sexual experiences, upon which I became fixated and for years and fantasized over. I would think of the sexual pleasure I derived repeatedly and would become increasingly aroused leading to more and more masturbatory experiences. Then I started using child porno to heighten my arousal for the same self-centered experience until I was caught. I have learned my lesson. I abhor my self deeply for my foolish ways in the past."

"Elijah, Elijah, have you heard the various explanations? Now get ready for the countdown for the answer you have for a long time searched for." The voice of the Revealer sounded as usual.

Then once again, just before he heard the voice of the Revealer, the same shadowy figure came past him for the third time showing his back with the words boldly written: ANACON. He never saw his face. A child with her head dangling just above the words was always seen crying for help.

CHAPTER EIGHT

COSMA SECURE UNIT- TREATMENT SESSIONS

On this occasion, having been found talking to himself and making statements to bust whoever killed his daughter, Bertha called his psychiatrist for help, who rushed to the family house. The moment Elijah saw the psychiatrist, he pointed his finger at him stating that the psychiatrist was the murderer and that he has come to finish the whole family off. "Come off, Elijah. This is Prof. Merck, your psychiatrist," Bertha assured him. At which he calmed down. He was administered a mood disorder medication, which caused him to sleep. On the hundredth day since being under sedation and monitoring for his mood disorder, Elijah fell into a trance for what will be his last time.

"Elijah, Elijah," the voice came back to him.

"The people you are about to see would appear to be mad, in the context of their behaviour, but as their treatment manager, they will tell you a lot of things that will inform you of the amount of technical knowledge they possess. Remember, though, that prison has its good protective element in the short term, but some prisoners can be exposed to sophisticated criminals and may come out worse than before."

Elijah found himself sitting at the head of an oval table with ten sentenced men. They each received at least ten years for their behaviour. Furthermore, they all progressed from watching pornographic images to actually having sex intercourse with children. Though, not all of them are University educated, they were very knowledgeable in computer technology, globalization, national jurisdiction, contemporary history and power politics and their impact on Internet pedophilia, which they took advantage of. Elijah examined some of the issues in detail, as explained by these offenders in order to assess the impact of relevant factors on risk management and to gain more light on the context within which such a phenomenon occurs and to have insight into other difficulties to be contended with when dealing with such Internet pedophiles in Metropolisia Cosma. The discussion was also to establish whether these factors have played a role in hindering or enhancing the cause of preventative measures. Elijah was mandated to challenge their mentality on all the issues they would raise. The treatment sessions were normally held from Tuesday to Friday, two hours per session.

Tuesday Session

Elijah, the treatment manager, posed the question: "Before the advent of computer technology, there was no mention of anything like Internet pedophilia. Since this phenomenon came into the public domain, the common catch phrase is "misuse of the Internet". Every police operation and consequent prosecution has involved evidence of indecent images found on a computer system with the Internet as the medium of distribution. An ex-convict, and former Internet consultant, who dabbled in Internet pedophilia by possessing indecent video clips and 4000 indecent images on his hard drive, and was recently jailed for 24 months said that the Internet is at the core of this phenomenon: an information source without limit, that cannot be policed, and whose content is determined by individuals as much as organizations. It is freedom that governments are quite keen to control. "So what features of this modern technology did you take advantage of and motivated you despite all the uproar and the hostilities that perpetrators face? But before we start any discussion you shall recite what you are."

In unison they proclaimed, "I am an Internet pedophile learning to respect the rights of the child."

"Good, make every effort to internalize this statement," Elijah encouraged them.

Stingray raised his hand and made a contribution. "Examination of the above scenario and almost all other cases of Internet pedophilia reveal a few facets of the phenomenon worth taking advantage of. The most prominent component is the fact that the Internet is simply an international network of computers linked up for the exchange of information between users or between a user and other services on the network. The second feature is the global demand for indecent images. The third facet is the availability of a medium for transmission of the material of concern such as the Internet Relay Chat room and an Internet Service Provider."

"What about these few facets that caused you to behave this way?" Elijah asked.

"I figured out that a way has been paved for me to get to some smart, but needy kids," Stingray answered

"Did it not occur to you that you may be misusing this important medium?"

"Having no other alternative to meet my needs, misusing a technological opportunity is the last thing that will come to mind."

"Stingray, think about it. You wanted to meet you sexual needs, right. Are you saying abusing the Internet was the only alternative to reaching the objects of your desire?"

"How was I supposed to know which child would beckon to my offer in my neighborhood or abroad, if I did not throw an anonymous line randomly? Is it not the same method people use in offering or seeking a product on the Internet?"

"That is right, but in the case you have just stated, people are able to make well-informed choices. Do you think hiding behind the Internet and reaching children gives them the opportunity to understand what is going on and reasonably consent?"

"Elijah, I cannot answer this, but I believe the new breed of kids are becoming smarter and thoughtful."

"Why are you not then considered a hero, but a villain, if your activities and that of your colleagues were acceptable?"

"May I chip in here?" Scorpion said.

"Yes, what do you have to say?" Elijah responded.

"I took my chances when I discovered that the Internet was an electronic, global and decentralized means of dissemination of information and knowledge. I also found it to be a powerful, instantaneous and interactive tool for strengthening both exclusiveness and inclusiveness and cultural diversity, the reasonable purpose of which is to benefit and to give power to Internet pedophiles, removing the barriers to the creation and the distribution of pornographic images throughout the world. Is it not wonderful that it makes use of very diverse techniques in a multimedia mode, including telecommunication, computing and audio-visual to provide pornographic images of children?"

"If I understand you clearly, were you of the mind that this fast and powerful system has empowered you to overcome all barriers surrounding children for their protection?"

"Somehow when it got into me that children may be of help to me, I was wondering how I was going to approach them until I realized what the Internet could do."

"What evidence did you have to come to the conclusion that to get to children, the Internet would be the best means?'

"I did not have any concrete evidence. It was impressed upon me that the unsupervised ones are also online and could be contacted this way."

"Why did you think a direct approach was not feasible?'

"Elijah, it would have taken a long time, and I would have been exposed quicker"

"Do you then agree that your activities were clandestine and illegal?'

"Well it is obvious from where I have found myself."

"I can see hands popping up over there. Is that you Vultura? Let us hear you," Elijah responded.

"Take a look at various aspects of human activity. Who wouldn't be motivated to get involved? The latest and up and coming technology stemming from ongoing research is unbelievable. This revolutionary wind has had tremendous influence on space exploration, mass media operations, medical technology, education, construction ventures, military warfare and underground operations like ours. Who here does not feel like his basic needs would be met by possessing relevant computer hard and software and going after kiddies technologically, if previous methods were risky and laid back?"

"Vultura, can you please reflect on your last statement."

"What do you mean, Elijah?'

"You sound like someone who has laboriously been on this game for a long time and looking for a means to expedite it?"

"Naturally, people become frustrated when things are not going as smoothly and quickly as they wish."

"Take a hard look, Vultura, do you sincerely believe that by finding the quickest and secure way of meeting your needs at the expense of children, their best interest would be served?"

"Let me stop you here before I forget. I have short memory, Vultura," Cobra interrupted. "What I want to say, though I am a man of remorse, is that computer technology has transformed the way we live, including the production of child pornography. Anyone with access to a computer and a modem can connect to on-line commercial services via the Internet. In this way the

Internet has quickly become the most significant factor in the sexual abuse of children and the principal means of exchange of child pornography. Through techniques of image capture, data encryption, anonymous re-directing through specialized service providers, images become increasingly mobile. I used some quite expensive user-friendly encryption software to make decoding of my files extremely difficult for others, especially law enforcement agencies to identify them. My recorded productions also became more and more live productions, whereby I raped children, tortured them, with simultaneous transmission to the computers of interested parties in my ring."

"From what you told us, where would you say your values, belief system and standards lie?"

"Clearly, the use of technology to reach those who would serve me as the occasion arises."

"Obviously, your goal was children to meet your sexual needs. Where did you get the idea that nature wants it this way? A grown-up like you and a kid for sex? Was it not slimy and shameful?"

"You have no idea how much effort I had to exert to get a single adult female."

"So what you are saying is weak as they are, you could take advantage of them without any resistance. Would you consider this as a fair game?"

"As you all ponder over my last question, the next question that needs be asked, bearing in mind the focus of the issues involved is, to what extent does this revolution or wind you are talking about impact on preventative measures that are in place, especially in Metropolisia Cosma?"

Without completing his statement, Croc pointed to himself to answer.

"I believe I can depend on my personal experience and perception here. There is evidence to suggest that in the past few years we have lived through a period in history, which can be described by a kind of lifestyle based on a new technological concept structured around hi-tech gadgets. This technological transformation process has created an interface between other technological fields through a common digital medium in which pornographic images are generated, stored, retrieved, processed and transmitted."

"I was even more aroused on realizing that features that form the core of what is described as the network society can be utilized to reach the joy of my hearts desire, kiddie sex. I found out that the technology that has brought on this network society is pervasive in the sense that it permeates every domain of human activity. This network society has become characterized by a set of relations or interactions that not only facilitate communication but also can be used to influence children or circumstances to one's advantage. The technology behind this position is also flexible in that it is able to adapt to a society or systems that are constantly changing. For example, the combination of words, descriptions and sounds in the same system, interacting from various points at a desired time along a global pathway affording ease of use does fundamentally affect the quality of communication with loose and vulnerable kids. This in turn, affects our culture or lifestyle, that is, our historically produced systems of beliefs and values. What has emerged should rather be called the interactive society. Is it not invigorating that communities in this interactive society could develop into physical meetings, friendly parties and supportive systems for members of their invisible pedophilic ring?"

"Surely, this kind of community can also be described as a group-specific electronic network of interactive communication organized around a shared interest of purpose, which, with respect to this discussion is Internet pedophilia. Hence, we Internet pedophiles do play roles and build identities online that defies preventative measures in place. Law enforcement officers will find it hard to trace us. Considering the way our activities create a feeling of community oneness and belonging and bring some comfort to people in need of communication and self-expression, should we not make every effort to maintain it? However, my experience also indicated that under certain conditions, use of the Internet sometimes increased the chances of loneliness, feelings of alienation, or even depression, as I became addicted and isolated myself. You know, life online can dehumanize social relationships and become an easy way to escape real life. Take a look at some marriages that have been ruined by Internet pedophilia. When it has come to that, we have risked being detected by the police, as we become vulnerable ourselves through our rejected wives."

"Croc, don't people hide their activities when either they are genuinely doing things that need privacy or doing something that is anti-social and shameful? How would you describe your pedophilic activities?" Elijah challenged.

"I have always been a private man. Which other manner did you think I would go about my business?"

"Would you advise your child to follow this private business of yours?"

"Dracula, you raised your hand. What contribution can you make?" Elijah responded to his raised hand.

"It must be recognized that virtual communities like pedophilic rings are another group of people with specific rules and dynamics, which interact with likeminded members of society and a community of helpless and vulnerable children. We serve a purpose and must be respected. For example, instead of the archaic and slavish family-bound and hypocritical culture of support and belonging that used to be practiced by so-called close-knit societies, one can define the present pedophilic entities as freedom communities, which comprise an individual's social network of informal and interpersonal ties, ranging from a few intimates to many weaker ties. Furthermore, I observed that most of these invisible community ties are specialized but serve many purposes, as participants build their products like pornographic images, videos and services of sexual relationship with needy children. Let me tell you, Elijah, that Internet pedophiles join networks or online groups on the basis of shared interests and values, and since they have multifaceted interests so are our online memberships."

"Dracula, I hear you talk a lot about building ties based on common interest. At their age, do you believe children's interest lies in having sexual relationship with people like you?"

"But we are giving them a hotline to address whatever needs they have."

"Don't you agree with me that you are rather taking advantage of their lack of understanding of the consequences of the activities involved and deceiving them?"

At this point, Shark raised his head to speak. "Yes, Shark, you have said nothing so far. Let us hear you." Elijah beckoned him.

"Considering further features of the network or interactive society, I can surely say that online life of pedophiles seems to offer advantages in that it is supposed to allow the creation of some relationship with children in distant lands or just a block away, supposedly on an equal footing in a pattern of interaction where personal and social characteristics play less role in framing, maintaining or even terminating communication. Hence, the Internet may contribute to broadening children's horizon in a society that seems to be in the process of rapid individualization and civic disengagement. I can also affirm that there is substantial reciprocal supportiveness even between a pedophile and a child, no matter how weak the tie is, which encourages unlimited and uninhabited discussion. Elijah, I am done. Thank you."

There were a couple of rounds of applause.

"Yes, experiencing the power of the Internet is eye-opening for children, but when you have achieved your diabolical goal of perpetuating their rape and emotionally damaging them, are you not rather facilitating their disengagement from society that betrays their trust?"

"I cannot answer this."

Elijah took over and summarized what had been said so far.

"In essence, what you are saying, and which motivated you were that pedophilic entities within this modern society have their own dynamics, with activities usually happening at different times; these activities combine the fast dissemination of mass media with the pervasiveness of personal communication, and allow multiple memberships in pedophilic rings. In relation to the focus of this discussion, the most important insight that can be gained relates to the technological infrastructure that has been put in place to facilitate the phenomenon of Internet pedophilia in this interactive society. You indicate that this infrastructure is a labyrinthine system, which can confuse most preventative institutions. A law enforcement officer becomes like a mortal man looking for a killer phantom (an elusive pedophile) to destroy in a dense and vast jungle of pedophilic activity. It may never be possible to find the weak points of this beast to attack, despite efforts to track it down. Furthermore, apart from the interactive society being pervasive, it is also elusive. Not only are your activities going on invisible to the naked eye or difficult to detect, but also clandestine. In other words, the information technology revolution has provided an indispensable means to usher in another set of lifestyles, which describe this era. You characterize these lifestyles as informational because your productivity and competitiveness in this society depend upon your capability to acquire up-to-date knowledge and apply your own intelligence-based information efficiently. You also term your lifestyle global because your core activities of production, consumption and transmission of indecent images are organized on a world wide scale, either directly or through a network of linkages between like-minded associates."

"Octopus, you said earlier that the idea of globalization touched your basic instincts causing you to take your chances. Can you please explain a bit further?" "Yes, globalization presents a better picture of the interactive society and sheds more light on how it impacts on preventative measures and Internet pedophilia." "The issue of Internet pedophilia and the factors that hinder or enhance it in the era of globalization cannot be understood properly unless the activities within Metropolisia Cosma, in relation to global operations in a networked or interactive society, are put in the right perspective. Is Metropolisia Cosma, and for that matter any country, aware that it has transited into a new world quite different from the traditional nation state? What moved me was a peculiar wind blowing across our world, which had the potential to stop the efforts of Metropolisia Cosma to control child pornography on the Internet."

"Whereas one of the major problems in the past was tribal wars and division, a myopic view of society, in this modern age a major set of issues at stake is that of globalization. This is the wind that is presently blowing across the whole world. The point is that globally active entities like pedophilic rings are playing a key role in shaping not only the economy of nations but also society as a whole. Don't you see how a lot of money is pouring in on our behalf, just to eliminate us? I cannot overemphasize that in this globalization environment can be found features, which encourage pedophilic activities and hence impact significantly on preventative measures." Foxy shouted in the group, "speak on brother. Say it loud and clear."

Octopus continued. "I need to make it clear that Internet pedophilia is a global issue, which needs international co-operation to control it. Whether it will be successful or not is another question. The features of globalization that I capitalized on to stifle the existing responsibilities and control apparatus of our beloved nation and militate against rounding up Internet pedophiles within her boundaries are not far fetched. The fact is that due to globalization, transnational corporations in the form of pedophilic rings are able to export activities to parts of the world where labor costs and workplace obligations are lowest and child victims, who are the raw materials, are easy to come by. Secondly, computerization, an important component of globalization, resulting in worldwide proximity, has enabled us to produce indecent images through a division of labor in different parts of the world and to break down and disperse these goods and services in a form of electronic entities. Thirdly, we are in a position to play off countries or individual locations against one another in order to find the cheapest fiscal conditions, in this case locating poor and vulnerable children and giving them incentives of whatever kind to entice them to participate in the sordid act, and at the same time look for the most favorable infrastructure, that is, places where child protection is very poor. Finally, in the jungle of global production, we are able to decide for ourselves our production sites. We do not need 20-storey buildings downtown, though sometimes we have availed ourselves of such luxuries. Indeed, this is a new phenomenon altogether to indicate that pedophilic rings, acting within the framework of what is called post-modern society, have gained additional scope of action and power beyond what Metropolisia Cosma can imagine or think."

"You have said a lot. Yes, globalization has given us immense opportunities. But what makes you think that your motive serves anybody's interest?"

"If we did not do what you speak against, the police officer would not be paid. Am I not serving the interest of some employers and employees?"

"Look at where you are now, look at public reaction, look at how some children have been affected. Don't you see complete selfishness in your behavior? On one hand you state that Cosma is your beloved country, on the other hand you state that you intentionally stifled its efforts on this front. Do you truly love your country?"

"Foxy, your encouragement to Octopus indicated that you have something up your throat to spew out. What is that?"

"Elijah, despite your questions, the inference to be drawn from what Octopus has just said is that the era of globalization has created an environment within which, like transnational corporations, pedophilic communities or entities can and do operate with impunity. Scrutiny of our activities points to the fact we are taking advantage of this new world society and are capable of evading regulations of any country. Our activities will always be beyond the reach of a nation state. On one hand, Cosma, for example, is a territorial state, whose power is based on a particular geographical location on this planet, where it exercises control over residents, current legislation and physical borders. The post-modern society which, in the wake of globalization, has taken shape is in many ways undermining the importance of Cosma, because an assortment of social circles, communication networks, market relations and lifestyles, none of them particular to Cosma, now cuts across the boundaries of our land. This impacts on law enforcement responsibilities too. This implies that, on one hand, it would have been better if Metropolisia Cosma kept to herself. On the other hand, such a move would get our country increasingly entangled in inconsistencies, restrictions and limitations as we would be shut off the rest of the world. Cosma must attract capital, people and knowledge in order to survive the kind of competition prevailing in this world society. This is where we Internet pedophiles take our chances. People think we are crazy, but we are very knowledgeable people, who are aware of this world society and its characteristics. We believe are also multinational entities, which comprise a number of business circles spread across the globe with a unique lifestyle of child abuse. We are aware that we are engaged in illegal activities in capitalizing on the advantages offered by the technologies within this new world society. You see, there is a striking similarity between multinational companies like MacDonald's restaurants, big oil companies like Shell, British Petroleum or Banks like HSBC and pedophilic rings. In all cases, individual units operate all over the world and are linked by various means of communication, including the Internet. The difference is that whereas one disseminates information about food items and provides food for the hungry, oil to pollute the atmosphere or money to the greedy, we relay indecent images of children on the Internet and feeds the illegal sexual desires of our associates. What is the big deal here?"

"Another characteristic of globalization is the lowering of the degree of internal social integration and personal inhibition. Hence, the social cement of this new society has grown so loose through the secular trend of individualization that society has lost its collective self-consciousness and capacity for united stand against child abuse. Stated otherwise, as the social scruples of the present network society and individuals have become eroded and weak, so have other ways of life evolved centered on freedom of some members of the community like us to express our desires by preying on helpless children."

"Foxy, I can discern from your words that you attribute pedophilic activities to globalization in a big way." Elijah challenged again.

"To what extent do you think you are personally responsible?"

"Surely, if the pathway had not been laid, I would not have known how to go about achieving my goal, no matter how sinister."

"You saw a way and you decided to follow it. Did some one force you to take that decision? If not, did you not know what freedom of choice entailed?

"Elijah, you mean priority, accountability and a sense of responsibility?"

"Exactly, and what do you say to this?'

"It appears my practice was at variance with my sense of social values."

"You have said it yourself."

Viper cut in and said, "I like this discussion, Elijah, because it tells you that though we are caged in here, more of our friends are still out there outsmarting law enforcement officers, aha, aha, aha! Let me add this. In emphasizing a transition into the new world society, as against the previous stand-alone Cosma, another notion of the phenomenon pertains to a state of society in which the notion of enclosed spaces is virtually non-existent, and where no country or group can shut itself off from others. Realizing this, it occurred to me that Cosma could be a place to launch special and clandestine social relationships, which is not integrated into or determined by individual national politics, and in which there can be invisible multifarious activities beyond human understanding. Hence in Cosma, realizing that nothing that goes on can be described as a local event, and Internet pedophiles like us could reorient our minds and re-organize our lives and actions along a global cum local perspective, we struck. You could not tell with ease whether the images came from outside or from me. Is this not fascinating?"

"Can someone then describe you as double-faced and deceptive?" Elijah asked. "Croc, were you going to make an addition?" Elijah asked again.

"Yes, by way of summarization. This state of affairs within the issue of globalization can be further interpreted as the processes through which other sovereign nations could be criss-crossed and undermined by well-informed Internet pedophiles like us with varying prospects of technological power, orientations, identities and networks. These processes brought to life transnational social connections, gave me a new way of looking at Cosma cultural values and facilitated this latest belief system of engaging in kiddy sex. In the same manner that these multinational entities, be it oil companies or banks, operate beyond the control of a nation state, so do we pedophilic communities conduct our affairs. We are equally affected by the factors that hinder or enhance globalization; namely, the extent of our operation and confidence, the number of connections in our global relationships and our self-determination through telecommunication. In other words, even as this world society is not a federal society, which encompasses different provinces or states within itself, but a world horizon characterized by multiplicity of events, including Internet pedophilia, I captured the unique opportunity of getting involved with children anonymously."

"So you have a belief system of sexual intercourse with children despite your age? What is the origin of this belief?" Elijah came in.

"Learned behavior from good friends. Simple."

"Peer pressure, right? How good are these friends who have caused you so much anguish by trapping you here and causing you to lose you dignity?"

"Can I come in here, please, Elijah, as I may forget."

"Go on, Stingray." Elijah said.

"Putting it in another way, a recurring feature of globalization is its refuting of the idea that we live and act in self-enclosed spaces of national states and their respective national societies. It means that borders become markedly less relevant to everyday behavior in the various dimensions of technology, transmission of pornographic images and our post-modern society. It also means acting and living together over distances across the apparently separate worlds of national states and cultures. This, in effect, allowed me to initiate my pedophilic activity or behavior no matter where I found myself on the globe."

"This is contrary to the traditional perception of society, which states that members of societies must be subject to state control of their land, sea and airspace, under the defensive authority or power of that nation. In this context, we would have been expected to be under the influence of Metropolisia Cosma government and to kowtow to her slavish laws and values. On the contrary, transnational pedophilic activities in the electronic medium defy the laws, which define activities in the local realm that are known in the national concept of society. We believed that this new world society would offer us new forms of life and action based on the special ability of players on the electronic frontier to maintain social links with children, which defy physical distances. In this era, there is an infrastructure within which a blend of activities occurs that seriously hinder national states in their claim to exercise control and order within their borders. This is the same era within which Internet pedophilia operates. Clearly, the fact that through police counter-operations, some of us have been located in various parts of the world attests to the truth that there is a technological infrastructure, which transcends national boundaries, through which we pedophiles are very active."

"You believed that this new world society would offer you new forms of life and action based on the special ability of Internet pedophiles to maintain social links with children?" Elijah asked.

"It appears that almost all your actions were based on some weird beliefs." He continued.

"I am forced then to ask you whether you and your colleagues have the right attitude towards children, respect them and believe that as much as possible their opinion on matters concerning them must be sought?"

Dracula, who boasted of vast knowledge on issues of national jurisdiction, raised his hand to make a link.

"Another facilitating factor of globalization is that, in this environment, civilization has left behind the age when national states knew all that was going on in their country and could exercise authority. Here, I saw the technological dimension and the dynamics of globalization as the platform from which to launch forth a multinational politics out of Cosma-based politics. I saw the possibility of this in the context of loss of government supremacy and emerging technology that have so greatly diminished geographical and social distances witnessed by faster and faster means of movement of goods, people and messages across space and time than ever before. It has been a situation that has fostered an interdependence of local, national and international communities that is far greater than any previously experienced."

Let me help Dracula here," Cobra raised his hand.

"In another way, one can describe the present state of affairs to the effect that national politics has lost its core power, which is sovereignty. Consequently, a new set of forces came into play that combined to restrict the freedom of action of governments and states by blurring the boundaries of domestic politics, transforming the conditions of political decision-making, changing the institutional and organizational context of national power, altering the legal framework and administrative practices of governments and obscuring the lines of responsibility and accountability of national states. These processes alone gave us the impression that the operation of states in an ever more complex international system both limits their autonomy and impinge increasingly upon their sovereignty. In this era of globalization, any idea of influence, which interprets as illimitable and indivisible form of public power is a mirage. I quickly took advantage of the confusion."

Elijah stepped in.

"Considering the harm that you are consistently posing to the international community, would it be right for me to say that anyone with eyes to see what the world information structure has to offer should be put to fright? The fear I can see is more abuse of children through you using a medium, which, as you describe, national governments have limited power to control. You state that the nature of the established infrastructure can be explained as a global information structure that uses the advantages of digitalization and fosters the networking of all communication services. In particular, it promotes the link-up of three fields of technology: the web-camera, computers, and the satellite, which come together in a multimedia structure, in combination with the Internet. You also indicate that if the newly acquired infrastructure is to be of relevance to users, it must be possible for information, of which illegal images of children are a part, to circulate around the world without hindrance. But, don't you think that in the advent of Internet pornography, Cosma has no alternative but to make every effort to prevent the abuse of such rights, contrary to the wishes of your colleagues, who are working hard behind the scenes and would wish that pedophilic images of any kind circulate without opposition?

Scorpion responded. "You may be right, but we have already spoken at length about the nature of the boundaries between countries. I must add that of all the forces eating them away, perhaps the most persistent is the flow of these images that governments are doing whatever they can to oppose, but with real difficulty. Today, people everywhere are more and more able to get the information they want directly from all corners of the world."

At this point, Elijah took over and summarized as usual. "What you are saying in essence is that, as the influence of national state at the electronic frontier declines and with it the loss of its meaning and reality, the notion of the interactive society steps in. It is an environment within which all lifestyles including child abuse on the Internet come together to play beyond the anticipatory power of the national state. It ushers in a difference in power between visible governments and invisible spectrum of pedophilic activities that affect the implementation of transnational law and the fight against Internet pedophilia."

"Having described the nature of the new world society as brought about by globalization, and the momentum it has gathered, the question is whether everything is going to be left to the whims of globalization without any effective control of a nation state. Don't you see there is a growing need for a binding international regulation, international conventions and institutions that must cover cross-border transactions? Furthermore, even as you indicate remorse, don't you envisage a better policy co-ordination among sovereign national states, better international supervision of activities like Internet pedophilia, closer collaboration within international organizations and strengthening of relevant children's organizations to ensure greater effectiveness in protecting children? Think on these issues. We shall continue tomorrow." Elijah pronounced the day over.

CHAPTER NINE

WEDNESDAY SESSION

They went through the normal routine before every session starts. They are expected to state in unison what they are: "I am an Internet pedophile learning to respect the rights of the child."

"I believe I can ask Cobra to express his opinion on the impact of the information technology infrastructure on enforcement of law across borders. I realize that it took a long time before you were caught, and I believe it was because it took sometime before law enforcement officers caught up with you over the infrastructure you spoke about earlier." Elijah introduced the session.

"Yes, of course," Cobra replied, as he took the microphone.

"As regards the issue of national jurisdiction and international enforcement of laws, I quickly became aware that within the context of the global information infrastructure, the policies within national regulatory mechanisms with regard to pornographic images that are emerging would always meet similarly bogus enforcement efforts. This is because the international dimension of the information infrastructure weakens the regulation of pedophilic images and free speech protection at the same time. Whereas on one hand democratic society is advocating freedom of speech, on the other hand, secretive pedophilic rings are working very hard to abuse this freedom. In other words, no matter what effort is exerted by Cosma to enact regulation or implement some preventative measures on her own, the preventative endeavours are unlikely to be as effectively enforceable as she desires."

"What I do observe is that the nature of technology concerned would compel nations to strive for international co-operation and partnerships in their preventative measures. But it is so clear that the global activities of Internet pedophiles, described so far, having been made possible through the creative features of the Internet, which has been empowered to make nonsense of distances, could not be stopped in successfully blurring and transcending political boundaries in the process. This would create an enormous potential for disorder within national political and legal arrangements and be a means to frustrate these collaborative efforts."

"This computer-based communication medium cuts across territorial borders, creating a new realm of human activity; namely, Internet pedophilia, and undermines the efforts to apply laws based on geographic boundaries."

"It is well known that state laws are regarded as territorial, and are expected to be different within other territorial borders. However, since this new phenomenon defies physical boundaries, different techniques and regulatory tools should be employed at the associated electronic frontiers. In any case, present law-makers and law-enforcing authorities still find this new environment unpredictable."

"One other factor affecting physical boundaries and law-enforcement is implicit awareness," Cobra continued. "When one travels from Cosma to another country, there is a general presumption that the traveler would be aware of possible change in the laws when the boundaries are crossed. However, in the realm within which Internet child pornography operates, these boundaries are insignificant. The rise of the global computer network has eaten away the link between geographic location and the power of local governments to assert control over the behaviour, the global computer network has eliminated the effects of government action on illegal activities, and it has undermined the power of a local sovereign to enforce rules applicable to such global phenomena. The result is that in the interactive society, it can be stated that natural borders are increasingly disappearing when it comes to pedophilic activities and many other computer-based activities. The Internet serves as a platform for multifarious trans-national unregulated interactions and services. In this light, any idea of unique cultural values of a particular geographic could be considered obsolete since the Internet environment allows different values and ethics to interplay resulting in global child abuse. It is a sphere of activity that is autonomous, sovereign unto itself and widely independent of state and national regulation."

"Do you see how cockroaches and other animals run into dark places when light is suddenly thrown on them? They instinctively know that they could be in danger?

Do you observe any similarity with your activities? If so why do you believe you would be in danger?"

"I think because society thinks our activities are dangerous."

"Cobra, you give us an impression that you became convinced that you could cover your trails in your child abuse efforts because law enforcement officers would not have the capability of tracking you down, is that right?

"Yes, Elijah. Though I knew a few people were being arrested, I was of the opinion that I was smarter than all of them. I was right for a long time."

"So what lesson have you learned since your arrest?'

"Considering the pain the coppers went through before my arrest, I am beginning to think that they are coming up to scratch, my colleagues out there would need to watch out."

Elijah interrupted and asked Vultura what additions he wished to make, as he raised his hand.

"What Cobra said implies that the global information infrastructure has a potential to pose fundamental challenge for effective leadership and governance with regard to policy-formulation and implementation. Policy makers and private sector organizations are searching for appropriate preventative strategies to safeguard and direct the some activities in the interactive society. But most attempts to define new rules for the development of the network have relied on unworkable concepts of bounded territory and nation state, ignoring the fact that the new networked society and the technological in use transcend national boundaries."

"So Cobra, what new rules should be made that has not been made?"

"No new rules or laws need be made. Unless our minds and hearts agree that children's and Cosma's interests are not served by our activities, and that we have missed the true objects of our sexual goals, society's efforts would have minimal effect."

Shark lifted his head to be given the chance to speak. "All I can add is that a new way of thinking should go into preventative measures that recognize the complexity of the new society, building constructive relationships among the various participants and promoting incentives for the attainment of the various child protection objectives. Regulation of Internet pedophilia, then, should not be considered as the duty of Cosma alone. The phenomenon has become global and interactive to the extent that its control must be seen as the duty of a complex mix of state, business, technology and the citizen. Normally, the restriction on dissemination of information of whatever nature can be enforced directly only within the territory to which the laws apply. But, the pedophilic activities going on in the current networked is almost impossible to restrict because when images that are passing through a medium are known to be illegal in one country, pedophiles easily transfer its transmission to another country with no similar prohibitions and the operations effectively re-deployed within a short period of time. Furthermore, because distances from a location of image sources are of no consequence to the recipient, relocated information source become easily accessible. Not only can pornographic images of children be easily re-deployed across porous national borders, but also, as stated before, by virtue of anonymous re-routing and encryption technology, perpetrators of such illegal material find every way to circumvent any national attempts at regulation."

"I have something to say," Dracula spoke up. "Echoing previous factors upon which physical boundaries relate to enforcement of law and suggesting the reasons why in this interactive or network society, preventative measures against Internet pedophilia by nation states could be limited, a further factor can be espoused; namely, powerlessness of government control. We know that control over physical space, the people and the things located in that space, is the defining attribute of sovereignty and statehood. This is embodied in law-making and law enforcement and the ability to impose coercive sanctions on law violators. In addition, an independent authority is characterized by the ability to claim personal jurisdiction over a particular phenomenon like Internet pedophilia or a diabolical entity. All these depend on that entity's relationship to the physical jurisdiction over which the sovereign has control. If there exist activities of, for example, pedophilic entities that are directed towards children within the jurisdiction, it makes sense that national sovereignty makes effort for that activity to be brought under control by that nation. At the same time, the law chosen to apply to Internet pedophilia should naturally be influenced primarily by the physical location of the action in question. In relation to the focus of this discussion, the implication is that with the source of Internet pedophilic images possibly coming from outside Metropolisia Cosma, the power to enforce the rules would certainly be significantly reduced."

"Scorpion, you have not spoken for a long time. Do you want to say something?" Elijah asked.

"Let me think. Yes, just to shed further light on what my colleague has just said. The other factor is the effectiveness of the rules being enforced. This is because the enforcement of regulation is exercised where that illegal activity took place. That is, the laws governing a particular behavior are most effective when the behavior occurred within the boundary where the laws have jurisdiction. In other words, as the primary source of Internet pedophilia could originate from outside Cosma, but residents of Cosma being only consumers of the product, national law is incapacitated in its full jurisdiction over this illegal activity, rendering law enforcement ineffective."

"Yea, Foxy, we want to hear from you again." Elijah motivated him to speak. "The third factor that can be cited is respectability or the authority of the law. It is generally assumed that residents within a geographically defined border are the ultimate source of law-making authority for activities that affect them. Within this border, those subject to a set of laws are expected to have a role in their formulation, and to be located in particular physical spaces. Likewise, government officials are given responsibilities based on the fact that physical proximity between the responsible authority and those directly affected by the law will improve the quality of decision-making as well as a desire to abide by the rules set, and that it is easier to determine the will of the people in physical proximity to the decision maker. It is clear that not all of the perpetrators of Internet pedophilia reside in Metropolisia Cosma, in which the offence is criminalized. Hence, the issue of proximity and its advantages will not count in expecting these external perpetrators to abide by the preventative measures in place in Cosma.

Elijah summarized the speech given on sovereignty thus: "we are in the age of information technology, which has unique features ushering in an interactive and networked society. This has resulted in globalization, which is undermining the efforts of nation states to control Internet pedophilia, and has resulted in the virtual non-existence of physical national boundaries. The implication is that pedophilic images are given free rein to move from one nation to another through a sophisticated technological infrastructure. This state of affairs has affected the effectiveness of leadership of any country. Within this networked society, preventative measures by a tiny nation like Cosma alone would be difficult, ineffective and woefully limited. An international partnership is the answer. I believe that other factors interplay to affect the regulation of Internet pedophilia, as those of you knowledgeable in contemporary history and politics are yet to discuss. Information technology, I must say, is the most recent tool used to perpetuate the abuse of children. At the other extreme end of chronology is the historical and cultural environment, which, over a period of time, has moulded belief systems until now. If any of you were motivated by issues of the past, tomorrow will be the day to say something. We are done for today's session. Thank you for attending and actively participating, but ponder over this question: by your activities, are you helping to produce a new generation of people who would have the peace of mind, the strong character and an environment to keep Cosma one and prosperous?" Elijah ended the day's event.

CHAPTER TEN

THURSDAY SESSION

"Let us recite what we are and hope to achieve," Elijah started the session. They, in unison shouted, "I am an Internet pedophile learning to respect the rights of the child."

Elijah continued, "If any of you were motivated by issues of the past, today is the day to say something."

Viper raised his hand to speak.

"Yes Elijah, I must say that child abuse, in all its manifestations, is not a new phenomenon. It has occurred throughout history for a variety of reasons and in different forms. It is society's awareness and concern which is new. I justified my action based on historic child abuse. Experts on child abuse agree with me in espousing how historic attitudes towards children have provided an unlimited supply of images and events, which have culminated in an entrenched diabolical belief system upon which children are still abused. Analysis of historically contingent factors involving abusive practices and attitudes serve to underscore how some of my colleagues and I continue to abuse children. If the analogies on which these parallels are premised are within limit, the comparison between historical behavior and our present behavior should yield some interpretative patterns that can be carried over from one period to another and enable us to uncover a certain continuity of features and structures between the two worlds. In effect, I wish to tell you that there is behavioral continuity between abusive attitudes towards children in the past and that towards children at present."

"The image of the child, as perceived in today's society, differs markedly from the images held at various points in history. So many years ago, as I gathered and believed, there was awareness of a difference between the world of the child and the world of the adult. Some form of preparatory education or initiation marked the transition between the two, but somewhere between that time and the present times the situation changed drastically. At this point, the idea of childhood as a separate stage of life, with its own characteristics, simply did not exist. The baby was hardly considered human, but maybe a little animal, and the toddler was a small-scale adult."

"Infancy in the past was described as a period of significant indifference, when babies and small children didn't count much emotionally in their parents' lives, but were treated kindly enough. They thought of them as small, immature adults, and as soon as these children could live without constant care, they belonged to adult life. Hence, children wore adult clothes and shared the games, toys, stories, work and sexual jokes of adults. This is unlike today, where age is used to define a person's role, behavior and status in society, where age is part of an individual's identity and many things are done according to our age group. However, it appears that some members of present modern society, including myself, lacked this consciousness and subscribed to the perception of the unenlightened times of the past and involved children in activities reserved for adults. I got swayed away with such a notion. Habits die hard, you know."

"Stingray, what do you have to add?" Elijah called him.

"One other attitude towards children was the fact that they were useful possessions for the family. In wealthier homes, they were important in negotiations for marriage, which could bring more wealth and prestige to all members of the family. The child's own feelings and inclinations were rarely taken into consideration. Parents also saw their children as useful bargaining items that could be used as another pair of hands to help earn the family's living. It was taken for granted that very young children worked, and as early as seven years they started their apprenticeship. The belief in the financial value of child labor continued for a very long time, during which time children as young as four could earn their own living. It was said of parents then that they brought children into the world to no purpose, if these children did not become contributors to the family purse as soon as their hands were steady. You have no idea how many of my immediate family members I abused and recorded to meet my pedophilic ring quota of a number images and to offer these images for financial gain."

Octopus stood up suddenly to speak.

"Though, the lack of consideration for the state of childhood began to change not quite long ago from today, the traditional indifference persisted until later times among many poorer and more rural families. Despite a series of social developments quite recently, among them, the emergence of the new-style entrepreneurial mentality, it seemed that at the same time the pattern of family life did not change much, as the quality of relationships of its members, both with each other and with society remained poor. During the war periods, relationships within the home had become more tense, and those between the home and the community much more fragile. Less social oversight of the family by the community and the loss of help normally inherent in the more collective way of life common in small communities meant that child rearing was more private and more intense. Though increased knowledge of child development and psychology led to heightened concern for the quality of parent-child relationship and to higher standards and expectation of parenthood, unfortunately, Cosma's practice or habit did not keep abreast with its knowledge, and socialization of children was still very much at the abusive end."

"This was evident by parent-child interactions at playgrounds and supermarkets. The amount of yelling, scolding, slapping, punching, hitting and threats meted out by parents on very small children was shocking. In such a culturally acceptable environment, impatience is easily expressed roughly, or even violently. Compounded by zeal to be seen as having children who behave very well, even in the face poverty and the associated exhaustion and depression, parents' ability to distinguish between discipline and harshness became easily blurred on most occasions. The economic and social developments which had improved standards of living, and helped to form a changed image of children and parents, also brought varying degrees of new strains and stresses." "Physical discipline became the basis on which Cosma relied to socialize children, and the degree to which physical force was used varied widely. For example, armed with this mentality myself, I would show pornographic images to children and threaten them that someone out there was always threatening to take similar pictures of them and take them around unless they yielded to me, if they needed protection."

"Foxy, you seem to have a point of view to express"

"Yes, Elijah. I learned to have my own way with children based on the issue of historic infanticide. Let me explain. It was an act practiced in all sorts of societies. It still goes on in many forms. This was believed to have been responsible for more child abuses than any single cause in history, apart from possibly the times of the plague. Infanticide involved the infliction of body trauma upon a newborn child so as to willfully and knowingly cause death. This excludes the less common practice of intentional neglect at birth, or the ritual killing of older children. One may be expecting a baby boy, but a girl appears. One may be expecting a 'perfect' baby, but a baby with some defect is born. The rationale for this practice has also generally been either religious appeasement or reactions to prophecies of doom or collective or individual acts of faith and proofs of unworthiness or due to survival instincts and population control. However, the uproar raised by members of the community in response to such acts caused the powers that be in Cosma to appoint a group of people to inquire as to the best means to prevent the destruction of the lives of infants. Furthermore, long ago, parents sometimes maimed their children so that they could be used to beg or be sold to circuses. A boy's face may be mutilated by surgery so as to appear to be continually smiling. In some societies, children as young as five years worked sixteen hours at a time, sometimes with irons riveted around their ankles to keep them from running away. They were starved, beaten, and in many other ways maltreated. Many succumbed to occupational diseases, and some committed suicide; few survived for any length of time.

"Consequently, it was not difficult for me to prey on children to meet my sexual needs. My belief was that if my ancestors used children when it suited them, why couldn't I do the same thing? I took cues from historic trends. You all know I have some sexually transmitted diseases. I did not care having sex with children and recording it because my belief was that knowingly harming children was sanctioned in the past. Why couldn't I do the same? I even thought they would transfer their health to me. But I have learned my lesson now. My mentality was wrong." Shark raised his hand to make a contribution.

"In Metropolisia Cosma, interest in child abuse came to a head when some concerned people raised the issue of this Island seeming to be inhabited by marooned pedophiles in the past. Although it had always been stressed that abuse of children covered a wide spectrum, ranging from emotional rejection through physical neglect, which included failure to flourish and the more severe form of malnourishment, to the infliction of serious mutilations, the issue of severe child abuse became associated in the minds of many in the Metropolisia Cosma region with specific characteristics whereby the child is pictured as being repeatedly beaten by parents and regularly sexually abused both within and outside their homes. In effect, uproar arose because abuse was thought to have become a regular cultural and community practice that, in turn, was being imbibed by some members of the community over time. I became aware later that abuse was a learned behavior and therefore, an alternative behavior could be learned. This could be achieved by reducing isolation and enhancing educative experiences, family exposure to and interaction with pro-social belief systems that can modify and discourage such abuse. This is our aim here with you Elijah, right?"

Elijah summarized the latest discussion.

"I must congratulate all of you who spoke for accepting that you held wrong belief systems and indicating that these sessions are teaching you a new way of thinking. In assessing the implications of historical and cultural factors for preventative measures in the context of the perspectives presented above, a few important points emerge. It appears that the abusive attitude of some adults towards the child has been that of blatant disregard for his human rights and has been inculcated based on precedence. Whereas some periods in history have been marked by understanding the rights of the child, most of the time the interest of the child has been disregarded. The child has not even been regarded as human enough, but almost a little animal or a useful possession for family use, whose consent on matters affecting him/her was not needed. It is my opinion that this notion persists today. The point here is that the old wrong perception of there being nothing wrong with abusing a child plays into the hands of you Internet pedophiles. If the perpetrator is of the opinion that what is going on today is what has been since time immemorial, then abiding by any laid down regulation would be meaningless to him. To him, abusing children is a norm."

"Secondly, there is every indication that historically most of the abuse of children have originated from within the family. It is clear that families make a lot of impact if they report these cases, and indeed it is they that face the brunt of the abuse. Hence, if the family is going to tolerate the abuse within it, or perpetuate it itself, then reporting would be minimal and efforts by preventative authorities would be undermined. If a question were asked as from where the present supply of children is coming, the answer would certainly be that the supply is not all from another land. The new material coming from on-line is of domestic abuse. On the videos seized by Cosma police, one can hear victims being instructed to imitate smiling daddies and uncles. Then follows the cries of the children during sexual abuse. Relevant national laws protecting children take into consideration the fact that most sexual abuse of children takes place within the home by people who are close to them. To reflect today's changing family structures, it would be relevant that laws that are formulated be widened to reflect the true meaning of "family" in order to bring under its umbrella those who would otherwise escape the maximum penalty for those in the position of trust. As well as blood relations such as parents, grandparents, brothers, sisters, half-brothers, half-sisters, uncles and aunts, the law must cover wide family members who are, or have been, living in the same household. This should include foster parents and foster siblings, step-parents, cousins, step-brothers and step-sisters. People who normally care for a child and live in their household, such as lodgers who baby-sit must be included."

Elijah thanked the participants and made a final statement. "As you realize, hardly was traditional abuse of children discouraged than another form of abuse reared its head, which as noted above, has centered around the creation, possession and distribution of indecent photographs of children on the Internet. Along with the phenomenon have grown very concerted social and legal pressures. Attitudes are hostile and cold, as people find it hard to understand how men like you would go after their children clandestinely and there is still not an iota of idea to explain the phenomenon of trading in indecent photographs of children on the Internet. You have become aware that presently, pedophilia on the Internet has become an experience that is severely and socially condemned as a phenomenon perpetrated by most people on this Island. Tomorrow we shall discuss the impact of contemporary politics on the phenomenon."

CHAPTER ELEVEN

FRIDAY SESSION

We shall continue our treatment session today with the exploration of other factors that motivated you to get into Internet pedophilia. Let us recite what we are and our aspirations. "I am an Internet pedophile learning to respect the rights of the child."

Elijah introduced the topic. "Having discussed some of the relevant past historical factors that contributed to the present attitude to the phenomenon of child abuse, including child pornography on the Internet, the question that needs to be answered today is: did the same society which is today decrying the depravity which lives within it, contribute in anyway, in the immediate past, to the emergence of the phenomenon? In answering this question, I would ask you to concentrate on social change, secularization and permissiveness of recent past. I believe the discussion will give further insight into the impact of long-held attitudes on preventative measures in Cosma."

Stingray raised his hand to speak.

"I am of the opinion that our current social ills originate from the hippie days, and that ever since, we have failed to recover from a period of moral decline or permissiveness that characterized that society. I believe my present attitude can be attributed to the decline of old time moralistic standards that was irresistibly taking place across our civilized society. Permissiveness has resulted from an imperceptible change in mentality that has been characterized by a nosedive of lifestyles into moral decadence and deterioration. It can also be described by a changing balance of power between some members of society and the declining influence of the conventional church. As a result of these changes and processes, Metropolisia Cosma must be described as morally diverse, making it increasingly difficult to maintain the stand that we live in an age where there is a general agreement as to how people should lead their lives. Before embarking on my behavior, I had the viewpoint that I can freely indulge in child pornography on the Internet, because I was in an age of unchallenged expression of self."

"My colleagues here will agree with me that in this perspective moral accord of any sort did not make sense, which fortunately or unfortunately has resulted in division, confusion and uncertainty in relation to values, belief systems and standards; this shift, being brought on by the whacko hippie lifestyle of yesteryears. Elijah, you and your cohorts, on one hand, advocate an orthodox standpoint, which desires us to go back to the old time biblical morality and to retreat from the present sexual and moral freedom or decay originating from the hippie era. You would be surprised how much I know. In the so-called puritan age, men accepted that the State had a duty to uphold morality and that personal values ought to be subject to the pre-determined standards of the time. In our liberal estimation, on the other hand, the old moral order is not workable in modern times, but that alone does not indicate that society must degenerate into a licentious abyss, though some changes are needed to commensurate with present way of life characterized by explosion of knowledge and new ideas. My colleagues and I are calling for increase in choice, which would ease restriction as well as individual frustration and fears. However, proponents of this view are also aware of the negative side of absolute permissiveness. There has been, for example, increasing crime rate. Typically, a series of infamous incidents in the immediate past and all the euphoria about our pedophilic activities on the Internet have been indicative of increased criminality, which resulted from permissiveness in the sense of emerging aggressiveness towards and disrespect for the right of children."

Elijah stepped in. "If all of you would agree with me, Stingray is indicating that you are beginning to appreciate the frustration of Cosma in general and parents in particular on the issue of Internet pedophilia."

"I think so," stated Shark, who continued the discussion.

"I got the whole idea of Internet pedophilia based on the confusion over morality with regard to issues pertaining to sexual deviance occurring then. Consequently, I entertained a wider and increasing doubt about Cosma's ability to exercise control over perpetrators like us, leading to a direct challenge to the authority of the State. Resulting from the hysteria and public reaction was a feeling of fear, displeasure and antagonism within Metropolisia Cosma, so that, whereas before the era this Island ruled mainly by unchallenged agreement on moral issues, it was now forced to rule by persuasion. Consequently, it became obvious that the ability of the State to mobilize popular support was diminishing. Hence, the method by which effective leadership was to be exercised moved from consent to coercion. In essence moral and social standards started to depreciate, catching all of us in the whirlwind."

Elijah called Scorpion, who indicated a desire to contribute, to speak up his mind.

"I know another standpoint from the legal and political elites. They view permissiveness resulting from some legislative maneuvering covering a period of between eight and twelve years prior to what appears to be the complete breakdown of society. During that period a number of key ethical issues were discussed by powers that be, resulting in a loose canon. Some of the discourse pertained to diverse conduct ranging from gambling and suicide to capital punishment, abortion and sexual activities, ushering in a kind of freedom of behaviour affecting social interaction, economic changes, relationships between genders and age groups, and the creation of new set of lifestyles. Thus the relaxation of the control of what was then regarded as unlawful acts may be seen as a direct response to adaptation to society's desire to think for itself. This may have been facilitated by major economic changes, increased social affluence and financial opportunities. What I am saying is that the ten-year period I mentioned represented the turning point in the move from the erstwhile public controlled life to the exercise of privacy in terms of moral issues; it was a move towards individualism and away from the rigors of collective disapproval through State controls. Since then there has been a battle between the two mentalities of liberalization and state control, doing things as one perceives right or as the public considers right."

"Viper, you said you had specific examples that would clarify the situation. What do you know or motivated you into such behaviour?"

Viper stood up. "What really moved me is the growing observation that in the immediate past, traditionally unequal groups (the young/the old; woman/man; heterosexual/homosexual and different races) were becoming less unequal in terms of power share. Before then, the less powerful groups, particularly, the young or women were not able to exert control and influence, and to articulate their own aspirations and desires. These developments resulted from altered social and economic relations, and the changes were expressed in new and different moral codes and values. For the first time, the young were able to express their views, which were at variance with traditional adult normative values. There were two consequences to this state of affairs. As sub-groups within society became more equal, the traditional moral consensus declined in favor of tolerance. Both society and its laws were placed under increasing pressure to reflect different values and moralities. So for me, a 45-year man having a sexual relationship with a 9-year old girl should not be a problem. We have become equal in power in this modern world."

"So Scorpion, when you were luring this 9-year old girl off the Internet for sex, how much did she say or do to indicate understanding or awareness of the consequences of what two of you were doing?" Elijah asked.

"I assumed that there was no difference between the two of us, and no matter her circumstances, I had to do what I had to do. I was of the firm opinion that at that tender age she was knowledgeable enough to understand the consequences of what we did."

"After what you have been through these years, have you come to a new way of thinking about you and a 9-year old boy or girl?"

"I have become aware of the limit to personal values. Furthermore, after studying human development in our previous sessions, I have realized that the extent of understanding of what goes on around us varies with age. A child of 9 may agree to do something by coercion but the activity may not be in her interest; neither would she be aware of the consequences. What I did was wrong."

"Croc, what do you have to say."

"The second consequence of hippie lifestyle is what is termed secularization, where there was an impression that the influence and importance of religion as the framework for moral guidance was on the decline. The long-established view was that Christianity was the basis of existing moral harmony and, therefore, as the impact and cohesion of religion declined, so too did the belief in a single cohesive body of moral rules. I personally formed the opinion that, if the church's authority was no more to be taken seriously, then I might as well form my own standards. This failure on the part of the church and orthodox religion meant previously accepted wisdom was unable to enlighten me with a clear, authoritative, single voice on moral issues, as it had once done. The church's traditional hold on representing the nation's morals became fractured. I was more impressed with the social elite who argued that traditional religious images, when used in our time, were out of date and irrelevant to modern society. I loved it when they said it was only failure to love, which was evil, and that morality should be determined by the relationship between people at particular times and particular situations. I believed sincerely that what I did with children was giving them love regardless of whether or not there was a perceived harm to them. What I am saying is that the two factors of changing power relations and secularization gave rise to the emergence of new liberties, including the freedom to engage in sexual relationship with children in whatever form, reflecting a system of moral pluralism, rather than moral consensus."

Elijah once again summarized the session: "An insight drawn from the above discussion relates to a historic, and what seems to have become a culture of depravity, permissiveness and lack of moral standards. In that sense, and for all the points raised, some of you would have a learned disposition towards abusing children and would have seen no point to recognize the right of the child to self-worth and dignity, and in the era of the Internet, and contrary to preventative measures in place, would continue to engage in Internet pedophilia. In addition, the suggestion is that perpetrators are of the perception that their behavior is the best alternative means of sexual satisfaction. They regard any form of regulation as an interference with their rights as they are of the opinion that modern society allows them to do what is right in their view without anyone questioning them. You would know by now that these tendencies are a challenge to regulation, as people of your mindset will always act contrary to any preventative measures in place. But you have promised to go out and respect the rights and dignity of the child after realizing that children's best interest is not being served through perpetuation of Internet pedophilia. You agree that you have been systematically raping them, but you have become aware by your presence here that justice will always be on their side."

At this point, after another ten continuous days of sleep, Elijah was officially declared to be in a coma, as he would not respond to any external stimuli. However, his brain was found to be very active. It was becoming a matter of concern. The last thing he saw just before coming round was this shadowy figure without a face. As usual a crying child's head was hanging just above a word, which this time read fully and meaningfully: ANACONDA. He also saw a tattoo of a huge snake with a widely opened mouth just pointing toward the child's head, as if about to swallow the head. This was on the shadowy figure's back. Then suddenly, he opened his eyes to the joy of the medical staff. He was shouting anaconda, anaconda, anaconda. Having narrated what he vividly saw in his trance, and having been told about police progress on the hunt for the killer of his daughter, he became convinced that he came out of his coma to witness and be part of the capture of his daughter's murderer. Does the culprit have a nickname, ANACONDA, as either a picture or word on any part of his body? Intelligence Officers got to work, hoping to combine scientific knowledge and information obtained from this remarkable vision.

CHAPTER TWELVE

THE EYE OF THE HAWK

It was 8:30 am in Calgary. The Head of Intelligence received a phone call from the Minister of Internal Protection that the Premier was concerned about public reaction to Internet pedophilia and some information must be received from law enforcement officers to be conveyed to the public about efforts being made to curb such incidents. This will allay the fears of members of the public. Alexia Denford, the Calgary-born world-renowned journalist, and a regular feature on the television program, Crime Awareness, was summoned to make the relevant contacts for the TV. She took it upon herself to interview two law enforcement officers who were known to have thorough knowledge of Internet pedophilia and were deeply involved in the present case, to shed light on how preventative measures and the efforts they are making to that end seem to fail, despite all the reported resources placed at the disposal of agencies fighting the phenomenon. She came on national TV to discuss her findings.

"Analysis of information I gathered from law enforcement agencies in an interview reveals five steps underway to bring Internet paedophilia under control and which impact on preventative measures," Alexia said.

"These are the operations they have to run to arrest suspects of Internet pedophilia, confiscate their computers, bring them to justice, if convicted, and ultimately subject them to rehabilitative measures; secondly, training sessions held by intelligence agencies; thirdly, monitoring of dedicated Internet channels; fourthly, co-ordination/co-operation with other agencies and finally, securing more financial resources. Let us now turn our attention to what they have to say." The two experts on the phenomenon appeared on TV through teleconferencing.

ALEXIA: You receive and give information about child pornographic materials to Hotlines, Internet Service Providers and the Courts. In co-coordinating your activities for efficiency what factors are paramount?

National Crime Busters (NCB): Giving and receiving is fairly a very small area of our work and the understanding of it is limited to a small range of agencies. We do not actually deal with Hotlines. We have got the Internet Watch Tower as a reliable place for information. We deal directly with Internet Service Providers and we will go through their point of contact or law enforcement point of contact. One of the difficulties we have on the police side is that instead of a single point of contact, we have a lot of police officers talking to us. So we use our normal processes to ask them for information. This means knowing who you are dealing with is the most important thing. This necessitates building up personal relationships in order to be able to phone somebody.

Personal acquaintances will phone me directly and say, "I have got a problem, what do you think about this?" What we have not done is get people in the police service updated with information on how the Internet works with regard to this offence. With the Courts, we even have greater difficulty. There is very little understanding in the courts of the Internet, and Operation Catch All will be the first time that the Jury will be made fully aware of how the Internet works and to explain what a chat room is and how images are transferred. With respect to establishing a four-way unit between a hotline, police unit, ISP and the court, it is possible but it does not exist in many things. Things happen in isolation, and when something happens we go to a local court and if it happens that you know somebody you are lucky. We have built up a relationship with the local Crown Court because of Operation Catch All, and for other work we have done we have gone to the same Judge because we don't have to explain the mechanism repeatedly. The Judge would have known what we are talking about. The only partnership-type form that exists is the Foreign Office task force, which is at a very high strategic level. There is nothing lower at a regional level.

Greater Regional Police (GRP): It is quite a broad question and it depends on who we are dealing with. It may be the local Hotline, the Internet Service Provider (ISP) or the Courts. The overriding principle of all we do is the fact that effective child protection is in place. And when I say child protection I mean, is there a suspicion about whatever we are doing when we contact an ISP, or when we get information from a Hotline or maybe when we go to the Courts for a warrant? Is there a child at risk? Are we just dealing with images or a child at risk? Child protection is the paramount issue. Secondly, there are other issues kicking in when we talk about efficiency. There may be issues relating to the material itself because the material is very sensitive in itself, and we have to be very mindful of the impact of that material on anyone else who actually sees it or hears of it. For example, we will not release material to the defense attorney. We will say to the defense that if they want to see the material, which we allege their client has, they will have to come to us to view the material on our site. The situation is different in most other scenarios where the police is expected to disclose evidence in its totality to the defense attorney. Because pornographic images of children are a sensitive material we will not release it without a Court order. It pertains to the right of the child who is being abused, who is being photographed and whose images are being shown and circulated to different people. There are issues in relation to the right of the individual with regard to who we show what to and when we show it, because that victim has been viewed many times already. By showing the images again, he or she would be victimized again. Lastly, there is the legality issue in relation to the material itself, as far as the Courts, the Prosecution Service, the Internet Service Provider and the Hotlines are concerned. The Hotline issue is a good example. Can people working with Hotlines who may access indecent images of children on the Internet lawfully possess them and distribute them even to law enforcement officers?

In terms of the link between us and Courts, ISPs and Hotlines, all I can say is that we have a more regular contact with our local Hotline, Internet Watch

Tower. They feed information to our Vice Unit and to the Serious Sex Offender Unit of the National Crime Information System. In terms of efficiency, it is early days in this province as it has been only a few years since these materials became very public and acted on. Certainly, when you go to the United States, I think they are further developed as they have got the National Centre for Missing and Exploited Children (NCMEC), which acts as a fully-fledged co-coordinator, and efficiency-wise they have got better systems than what we have over here. There in their unit, they have representatives from FBI, US Customs and law enforcement actually built in, and it is a centrally funded unit. The Internet Watch Tower is funded by industry so one might argue whether it is independent and whose interest it is actually serving. Is it looking after the interest of the children and those using the Internet or the group of industries that formed it; that is, the International Service Providers Association.

ALEXIA: The speed of evolution of Internet technology is presenting law enforcement with new technical challenges. What type of training in your opinion will be needed to keep pace with these challenges, and does it have international perspective?

NCB: As regards training requirement, I can confirm that there is some level of training at the moment and new training programs are being developed. The high tech unit has the lead in deciding what is required but we tend to learn as we go along. There aren't specific training courses on a crime like child pornography, for instance, but with time we have learned the art of seizing and handling data. It is not mainly about child pornography, but rather computer-based systems. It is about how data is stored, how we can produce it in an evidential form, and how to confirm that this computer was used by this person. So it is very much about evidence. Encryption is also an issue; how to look for encrypted files as pedophiles have started using these. With regard to international perspectives, this is vital because it is not easy to obtain information from international colleagues. This because Canadian criminals could be registered in the US with an IP address, so when you do a search in a newsgroup or chat room and see pedophiles distributing images to different people you are able to obtain the IP address and other details, but you actually need to know who is at the other end of the IP address. On top of this, you need to get the data from the US. The question is: how do you get all this in evidential form. You have to prove before a Canadian Court that the person is the one who is sending the images.

GRP: Yes, training is needed at all levels. We provide some training. If you look at the management of police organizations and others, you realize that we do some training for Probation Officers, for the judiciary and for the Magistrates' Courts. There is awareness training, there being the need to know in broader terms about the developments that are taking place and what pedophilic activities are emerging because of the Internet. There is also the need for them to be able to handle complaints and get a general understanding of what the complaints involve in relation to the allegation of material on the hard drive. And they need appropriate training to make sure that they are capable of seizing the material safely, because the worst case scenario we often get is that an officer may be called to an incident where there is an allegation regarding an illegal material on the computer. If they are not aware, they may switch the machine off and have a look at it. In evidential terms, that is the worst things we could possibly do because then we are interfering with evidence. The integrity of the evidence is maintained if the computer is just seized without switching it off, that is, just unplugging it and taking away. The highest form of training is staff being trained to do forensic analysis, including being able to know that no one has tempered with evidence. This can involve switching on the system again and inserting a floppy or attaching some peripheral. There are a lot of levels of training required. In terms of having international perspective yes, because the phrase I coined recently is that the Internet is "glocal" from being both local and global. We deal with materials and individuals locally, but by virtue of the Internet being instantaneous, the issues become global. Therefore from the training point of view, we have been involved in training with Interpol and Europol, attending training sessions and inputting into their training so that law enforcement could understand each other's difficulties. This is because whatever action we can take in Canada, the police officer in Germany or the UK may take a different course of action. We might be able to provide them with intelligence, but unless we provide it in a certain way, they may not action it because their law may be different.

ALEXIA: Which international or national operation would you consider to have been well co-ordinate? What factors do you consider might have made it more or less successful? What would you say are the implications for fighting child pornography on the Internet?

NCB: Operation Catch All is not the only one, but is the benchmark of such international operations. It was successful because we actually managed to get 12 countries to work together. So we got all the information we needed but realized that only 7 of the 12 criminals were operating in our locality. The rest were operating outside, and it was the co-ordination of the world-wide activity which was significant. I can say Interpol played a key role, but my predecessor managed the operation. It was a very painful process to have all 12 countries to agree. It had to be put off occasionally; dates were set but people were not ready; there were different priorities, different capabilities. It is time-consuming and needs a lot of commitment to do it. What we tended to do now is much smaller scale operations. It would have been less successful if we had not had the co-operation. We do need better laws; there is no doubt about that. In Sweden, it was a small fine for possessing Child Pornography. Portugal did not agree that such an offence existed in their country. In Scandinavia, they said they did not have a problem. They also deny that it exists. In America, Internet pedophiles could be imprisoned for 25 years. Canadians have difficult laws. There was a pedophile who said it was his right to look at such images if he wants to. This is his sexual preference.

GRP: Clearly the best ones are the ones we have run. We have been looking into the Internet proactively since 1995. Operation Stardom was run by Westland Police, and that was one of the first targets to be convicted in our area for possession of child pornographic material. The culprit was a managing director. In 1999, we run Operation Queenstown and Zimbel, and most recently Operation Nedal in March 2001. It was fairly co-ordinated but we went on that proactively. We told people at the National Crime Centre (NCC) what we were doing, and for Nedal we concentrated on national sites because of the software we developed. Operation Pathetral, conducted by NCC was very successful in terms of creating public awareness on the issue. For those which were less successful, it would appear it was because some countries that were expected to play an active role failed to do so.

Analysis of Interview

Alexia summarized the discussion.

"It can be inferred from the interview that multi-agency operations are in full swing to counteract Internet pedophilia. With regard to operations, many other instances were cited in addition to those mentioned previously. Successes in these efforts have prompted the government to create an elite cyber cops squad worth over $50million in personnel and technology to tackle computer crimes, including fraud aimed at national businesses, Internet sales scam and crimes targeted at the national infrastructure. The relevance of these efforts is that the government is improving the technical capability of law enforcement and regulators, and setting up an Internet Crime Unit. This can be deemed a practical way of co-coordinating expertise and ensuring clear lines of responsibility. This National Unit would be empowered to investigate the most serious IT crimes, act as a forum of excellence for deliberation on Internet crime cases and a source of support to other forces dealing with offenders who are adept at intricate computer crimes."

"These operations have indicated that an effective international co-ordination is possible, though some problems still exist. These include lack of efficient exchanges of information and ongoing co-ordination. Other problems are lack of infrastructure, and points of contact in foreign countries. There is also a need for secure communication systems and common databases. These cause delays in the co-ordination efforts."

"Faced with the challenges such as detecting Internet crime, which transcends state border controls, the material being transmitted being an intangible mass of information, possibly encrypted and of anonymous account and the medium of transmission being transnational, gathering evidence can be tedious. For these reasons, it was suggested that there is a need to possess adequate technical know-how to facilitate prosecution in a highly technical and fast-changing environment. There is also a need for comprehensive and ongoing training."

"On the contrary, it is observed that training facilities and level of technical expertise varies from one country to another. In addition, it appears that provincial/federal level units are better equipped than local levels. Lack of financial resources is blamed for this deficiency. With regard to its international dimensions, you heard that an international training symposium for law enforcers would not only raise awareness and know-how of the relevant issues but also encourage supranational law enforcement and international co-operation through personal contacts. Consequently, in various parts of the world, including this country, law enforcement units dealing with the phenomenon are regularly undergoing training to keep abreast with legal and technical changes. The findings would suggest that perpetrators of the phenomenon are working against all odds to feed their habit, but coercive powers of the state are equally active to thwart their plans."

"There is evidence from law enforcement agencies to confirm that majority of perpetrators operate through the Newsgroup area of the Net and chat rooms, and not the websites. This is because websites are easily traceable and no commercial sex site operator is going to offer child pornography because he knows that he will be shut down. However, patrolling chat rooms and newsgroup channels is a problem. They are difficult to police, as there is not enough police resources to monitor these chat rooms. Unlike the United States and Canada, police officers in many countries have limited powers and technical know-how to pose as youngsters in on-line chat rooms in order to track down pedophiles."

"Despite police's use of increasingly sophisticated technology, abusers are aware that the Internet affords anonymity. Police admit that tackling cyber-porn will get more difficult as technology develops. The recent pedophile ring incidents highlighted the complex and expensive nature of a police operation against a world-wide network protected by multi-grade encryption and password anonymity. As stated earlier, encryption, the technology that enables personal computers to scramble a file such as a picture or an e-mail so that third parties cannot read it, even if they use the most powerful computers, enabled members of pedophilic rings to evade police. A spokesperson from the National Crime Centre admitted that, "we were able to get into criminals systems when they voluntarily gave us their passwords. Once again, this reveals that there is more than the eye can see."

Alexia continued her analysis on TV.

"Using all means within the rule of law, law enforcement agencies have used manual, overt and covert methods, including special software to achieve their goals. These efforts have been the backbone of successes in national and international swoops on pedophiles. However, it is observed that the extent of Net patrolling differs from one country to another. For example, under the "Innocent Images" program, FBI agents have posed as children using false names in chat rooms, newsgroups and file servers. These undercover sessions take place in areas of the Internet where criminal activities are known to be sited. These schemes are not available in most countries."

CHAPTER THIRTEEN
ELECTRONIC RECONNAISSANCE

As Alexia planned from the start, she placed emphasis on the fact that she was seeking to understand the confrontation between risk managers and the public at large with respect to Internet pedophilia in this country in particular and globally in general, and to ascertain the impact of identified factors on resolution of the conflict. Based on her local and international observation, her conclusions gave further proof that despite all the efforts being made, control measures still face challenges, and that in this era of computer technology and globalization, these efforts fall short of expectation. She was invited by a local Calgary Court Service and then an American Supervision Unit to observe how Internet pedophiles are managed.

The National Court Service aids both in sentencing perpetrators and supervising those that are convicted and thus helps control Internet pedophilia. The acknowledgement is that the Internet child pornographer is as sexually depraved as any sex abuser. However, the cycle of abuse is somehow different, though they are equally behaviorally and cognitively distorted. In view of this, the Court Service makes child pornographers undergo specially tailored sex offender treatment program in the community. Using the therapeutic effect of group work and specially designed exercises, which is underpinned by cognitive-behavioral therapeutic techniques, their attitude towards the offence and any victims and their awareness of the feelings of the children involved are confronted and challenged.

Further analysis of Court Service efforts, as Alexia learned, reveals that for offenders, who have been involved in the criminal justice system and have been convicted, there is inconsistency in home visits for those awaiting sentences but live in the community. Because of the possibility of being made subject to a community rehabilitation order or eventual release from prison on license, it would be a flaw and a sign of negligence if their home circumstances are not assessed to ascertain, during the Pre-sentence report stage, that on return home, the public would still be protected from harm and that they would be in the position to receive treatment.

Evidence also suggests that as some Pre-Sentence Report writers are not well trained as semi-specialist officers, the quality and consistency of these reports are questionable and sentencing flawed. Furthermore, lack of reference to sections of relevant Criminal Justice Laws for extended supervision during community sentence or when on license could result in inadequate period of supervision. This implies that these offenders would not in the long run have their distorted thinking confronted and addressed effectively, causing them to re-offend.

In the same vein, she observed with concern that occasionally pre-sentence report writers have proposed community orders or fines for such abusers. This means there is no provision to address their sexual offending behavior, but leave offenders in the community, thus increasing the risk to the public. There are also concerns for child abusers to be given community rehabilitation orders or come out on license but who do not participate in sex offender treatment programs. Research indicates that these were twice as likely to be re-convicted of further sexual offences as those who had participated in a treatment program and were five times as likely to be re-convicted of further non-sexual offence.

As Alexia found out, there has been an increasing interest focused on the treatment of sex offenders, both in prison and in the community. However, there remains the ever-present problem of resources. Surveys of current practice of Court Service work with sex offenders conclude that cost was an important issue and one, which potentially may override all other considerations. It was pointed out that any mismatch of treatment need and resources allocation will diminish the potency of practice and may prove counter-productive. Given that it is essential that sex offenders were supervised to the highest standard and that breaches were initiated in every case, unless otherwise at managerial level, there must be serious concerns that the order was not being enforced appropriately in some cases.

Whilst it was not always advisable to end supervision abruptly when the order or license terminated, if the offender was willing to continue to contact, the period of voluntary contact should be subject to a risk-management plan, which included continued oversight from managers and plans for the withdrawal of the Court

Service and the final exchanges of relevant information with the appropriate agencies. However, there are financial implications, as there is no specific provision, in budgetary terms, for such continued supervision, nor does it form part of the existing expectations in Court Services. This also means that due to financial constraints, there are such abusers who are in the community with incomplete treatment.

Alexia also noted with concern that though the needs of victims are taken into consideration, along with a lot of factors connected with the prevention of re-offending, sometimes these assessments have resulted in a sex offender returning to an area where his victims live. There is no doubt that a remote chance exists for child abuse to recur. One reason is lack of housing facilities elsewhere.

Another sign of limitation on risk management is the fact that the notification requirements are imposed on only a comparatively small number of offenders who have either been cautioned or against whom a formal finding that they committed the relevant act has been made by a criminal court. This implies that there are quite a number of abusers out there who would still be left to their own schemes. Attempts were made to widen the scope of the provision by extending the notification requirements to those found in civil courts, industrial tribunal or disciplinary hearing. This is in line with Children's Charities Incorporation that the majority of children are not abused by convicted offenders and in minority of cases, where prosecution follows the disclosure of abuse, the rate of conviction remains very low.

As Alexia found out, comparative analysis of supervision of sex offenders in different parts of the world indicates that there are variations in the intensity of this activity. For example, in some regions of the world, there are dedicated units within the Court Service whose remit is to work solely with sex offenders. Every effort is geared towards supervision of sex offenders, and they do not concern themselves with other offences, which have no relation to sexual offences. Among these dedicated units are either civilian or police surveillance officers who spend their working times monitoring these offenders in the community. They have the power to enter an offender's house at any time and monitor their activities; to check whether they even have underpants on or are in possession of any sexually stimulating or sexually oriented material or children's clothing, toys, games and videos without prior approval of their Probation Officers. They are equipped with radios and emergency connections; they work evenings and weekends so that they may truly monitor how offenders are spending their leisure time and avoiding contact with children. However, there is a debate about the possibility of infringing on the human rights of these offenders. The counter argument is that their rights would not be infringed upon if they had respect for the rights of children. The inference is that regulators would have to come to terms with the special nature of this offence and dedicate their time and energy to combating it. The extent of focus can impact on how far success is achieved by Internet pedophilia control measures.

For example, in some parts of North America, where Alexia did ten days intensive participant observation, she observed that as a result of legal changes, the development of an intensive and proactive approach to short and long-term management of sex offenders has become necessary. Lifetime probation enables offenders to be assessed during different phases of their life. It also gives supervisors the time to work with difficult cases without being rushed to monitor reunification or to see the terms of probation expire for compulsive exhibitionists or pedophiles, knowing that they will re-offend. For some others, their own childhood victimization has been so severe and traumatizing that several years of work is needed before they can work through issues blocking their progress.

In addition, in view of the fact that sex offenders live a life of secrecy and deception and that traditional therapy requires a lengthy, painstaking and expensive process of self-disclosure, and still one can never be sure that the offender is telling the truth, it became necessary to use a polygraph. The polygraph may be used in two ways in the supervision of sex offenders. Firstly, as soon after sentencing as possible, a disclosure polygraph is required. In this session, the defendant first goes over all the questions to be asked with the polygrapher to examine in detail the offender's sexual history and history of sexually deviant behavior. Secondly, further on in treatment, the polygraph is used not only to monitor the offender's compliance with the restrictions placed on him but also to measure how he is managing his inappropriate thoughts and fantasies.

Furthermore, many programs use the penile plethysmograph as one of several components of testing and to help offenders in the behavioral reductions of deviant fantasies. She observed, however, that because of extensive controversy in recent years over the use of such a tool, the plethysmograph could only be administered with a doctor's prescription, and only audiotapes may be used for testing. On the whole, she realized that more resources and powers are needed to give the police and other control agencies more latitude in their operations.

Alexia then sought interview with Internet Service Providers, again through teleconferencing on TV, which revealed a number of loopholes but also opportunities to control Internet pedophilia. The collective opinion suggested that at least five major areas, which impact on control of Internet pedophilia, can be identified. The first focus was on the monitoring of activities on the Internet. The second point was the extent of co-operation between ISPs and other agencies in combating Internet pedophilia. The third focus was on the nature and impact of Codes of Conduct. The fourth related issue was the extent of user involvement in formulating the codes and complying with them. The fifth factor was once again inadequacy of financial resources, which she had emphasized over and over.

She summarized thus.

"With regard to monitoring activities on the Net, it was made clear that, unlike other public service regulators, the practicalities of scrutinizing server logs for abuse, as a matter of routine and thus call attention to compliance issues would be unimaginable. In addition, it is observed that ISPs may not be examining their server logs as often as expected because it would be taken as infringement on clients' human rights, freedom of expression and privacy. This means that questions of legal requirements for providers to hand over data of their clients to law enforcement agencies must be resolved. Furthermore, it is held that the Net holds a lot of data, which could also be heavily encrypted, to be practically feasible to examine, in view of limitations in terms of financial, technical and human resources. It is arguable that if it was feasible and abusers were brought to account and confronted, Internet Service Providers would fear losing customers. This is a possibility, which, it is feared, causes Providers to pretend nothing is going on. On the other hand, it is suggested that if Internet Service Providers had the resources to sample server logs regularly in order to reveal abusers, the public would be served better if Internet Service Providers informed these culprits to stop their illegal activities or risk losing their membership. This is the sanctioning step that is expected of self-governing systems and underlies their effectiveness and one of the reasons for being preferred above other systems."

"It could then be inferred that Internet Service Providers can play an effective part in controlling the phenomenon in question. Since Internet Service Providers were granted protection from liability, if material on their servers was not intentionally known to them, they have co-operated actively in identifying the abuser and bringing him to justice, thus helping in combating Internet pedophilia. Regulation is then facilitated if there is a good working relationship between ISPs, Hotlines and the Police. For example, when the police are told by Hotlines of illegal content to be investigated, and ISPs are also informed and asked to leave the material on their computer systems until any investigation is complete, relevant agencies would have co-operated by making it possible for server logs to be examined. By examining the e-mails and server logs of any websites that abusers used, law enforcement officers could find out who else shared their interest and when they were on-line."

Coordination

"Continuing with the issue of co-operation, there is evidence from the interviews that, in many instances, when ISPs have independently received calls on illegal materials on their servers, they have reported to their national Hotlines and in most cases informed callers of any actions taken. However, evidence also suggests that it is not all ISPs that furnish external agencies with required data on a perpetrator. This may be because they are blatantly refusing to co-operate, their system is not set up to record such data or they do not have the technical know-how to retain the needed information. Another factor, which has been cited already, is lack of good working relationship or co-operation between agencies. Obtaining feedback on how reported cases are being dealt with in different countries is very crucial. However, because of differences in priorities, financial capabilities, laws, languages and cultures, exchanging information and acting in a synchronized manner can be difficult and time-consuming."

"In conclusion, the evidence presented above implies that control measures have not always been successful. They have had only limited control over the actual behavior of individuals and institutions. Further specific propositions could be advanced to explain the limitations imposed on preventative measures."

Code of Conduct

"Whereas in some legal systems, codes of conduct are independent of national legal systems, much co-operation is encouraged with law enforcement agencies. In other systems, these codes are closely intertwined with the legal rules. She envisaged that out of these different codes could emerge an international law, which would become a worldwide law for Internet Service Providers. However, she became aware that one problem with codes of conduct is that they lack any legal binding capabilities for the provider and the user. But this could be rectified by incorporating the codes through a contractual agreement between the provider and the user. It then becomes a contractual enforcement of non-binding codes of conduct."

User Involvement

"The fourth major observation made from the interviews with ISP's, and alluded to earlier, is the importance of user involvement in formulating Internet Service Providers Codes of Conduct. Whilst it appears that some Internet Service Providers obtain much user input, others don't and expect users to observe their strict rules or policies without which they are struck off membership lists. The issue is that if the public does not feel part of any policy formulation or decision-making, they do not identify with the policies and hence do not feel like owning the rules and abiding by them. It is believed that associations of ISP's need to seek customer input in their policy formulation to help reduction of illegal activities. This also makes ISP's open and fair."

"Hence, it was suggested that a number of risks and limitations are associated with self-governing approaches, especially if they need to meet the aspirations of the public, as in the case of policing Internet content. In other words, the acquisition of power by groups that are not accountable to the public through the conventional lawful channels may constitute an abuse. Authenticity plays an important role within the debate about the potentials of self-governing. Part of the discussion is linked to the responsibility of mediating institutions to ensure transparency, accountability and consultation with interested parties. These are generally not perceived by the private sector as their primary objectives. Therefore, ensuring accountability when public interests are concerned should be a major concern in the design of a self-governing system. Furthermore, self-governing requires active consumer and citizen participation at all stages of development and implementation. It is envisaged that important aspects of transparency of self-governing institutions include the imposition of meaningful sanctions on industry participants, clarification of standards, effective enforcement of these standards and open and just sanctions."

"Those of you who listened attentively observed that since the actions of self-governing bodies directly involve public matters, it is important to emphasize the fact that the conduct of their duties must comply with principles on good standards in public life, which enshrines seven principles of Public Life. These are selflessness, integrity, accountability, openness, honesty, effectiveness and leadership. These principles apply to all aspects of public life and they are being emphasized for the benefit of all who serve the public in any way, including self-governing institutions. Accountability, effectiveness and openness of these regulatory players involved with the Internet governance are equally important as it portrays their respect for fundamental human rights of children. There was emphasis on the fact that all government and quasi-government child protection agencies should be accountable to the public, and that no decisions should be taken without proper public consultation and an open and transparent environment should be established for preventative initiatives in the field of Internet regulation rather than important policies being developed behind closed doors in secrecy. The public has the right to know from the very early stages of a policy-making process involving child protection. Apart from being accountable and open, the government and quasi-government agencies should be competent in the field of Internet regulation in technical, social and legal sense so as to provide the public with effective solutions, as it is being sought now following the abduction and murder of Mr. Morrison's daughter."

"In essence, Internet Service Providers are one form of self-governing industry that the public can look upon to develop industry-wide guidelines, a set of industry principles and practices that defines right conduct as it spells out the industry's public commitment to moral restraint and aspiration on the Internet. This general framework is collectively called Codes of conduct or practice."

"Acting in accordance with principles of social responsibility, Internet Service Providers have adopted codes of practice to ensure that they meet community concerns and industry needs and operate as an accountability system that guarantees a high level of credibility and quality. To be effective, these codes of practice have been the product of and enforced by the self-governing industry entities themselves, though often in collaboration with government."

"Generally, despite obvious shortfalls, Internet Service Providers have become formidable self-governing systems, which are playing a part in the combat against Internet pedophilia. Through their codes of conduct they can banish perpetrators and enhance preventative measures. They have also facilitated the prosecution of perpetrators of Internet pedophilia by allowing their physical addresses to be located, aiding their arrest. To a large extent then, Internet Service Providers have enhanced the control of Internet pedophilia. However, they could also be lax in meting out sanctions to violators."

CHAPTER FOURTEEN
THE LAST SENSE

Findings from the Internet Watch Tower (IWT) in this country, based on interviews Alexia conducted with officials of the unit, informed the rest of her discussion with regard to the activities of the Tower, nicknamed The Last Sense, that impact on regulation of Internet pedophilia. Once again, Alexia spoke with the experts on a TV forum:

ALEXIA: How has the fast changing technological environment enhanced or hampered your activities?

IWT: I guess it means we have to change fairly quickly to keep up in terms of our own software and some of the techniques we are using. That is not a great problem because we are supported by the Internet Service Providers who are the most technically advanced anyway. Our procedures are basically fairly low tech, as we don't need any sophistication to find content on the Internet/web. I guess one of the changes is the new service in terms of communications. One thing that has affected us particularly is live services like chat rooms, which does not fall directly in our remit because it is not something that can be reported or would have us to go and look at because it has already happened and gone. That means an increasing proportion of the problems on the Net is not within our remit. That is where we have developed more of an education and awareness role in recognizing that the problems arising from the Net are that the defence is not through probably removing it, rather parents and children be made to understand the danger and safety rules of the Net. So I think the technological environment means that our particular remit in what we do is gradually becoming less central in dealing with risks to children on the Internet. With regard to encryption, it is slightly strange, as it is not in public view that pedophilic rings are increasingly using encryption; but our remit is about what is publicly on view. If it is encrypted, it is not publicly available. It is problem for police in breaking into pedophile rings or exchanging files in encrypted format, but is not a problem for us because by definition it is not within our remit, and nobody can report it to us. The comment I have is, no matter the nature of encryption it remains effective as long as no one is able to crack it. So for police purposes once they establish that somebody is a pedophile or someone may have child porn pictures on their computer, they can usually find unencrypted pictures unless someone is careful and encrypts the unencrypted pictures. Otherwise, they can find unencrypted pictures at the end of the chain. So in fact some of the pedophilic rings like the W0nderland case, which came in as a big international prosecution, became known because police activities revealed addresses or e-mails with which perpetrators were identified. Anonymity on the Net is not what we concern ourselves with.

ALEXIA: Is there a laid down protocol when contacting other agencies in and out of country, and how easy is this co-ordination for effectiveness?

IWT: The procedure we have laid down here was studied and recorded and approved effectively in the government review of our services a couple of years ago... Since that review, we have been through what we call liaison meetings, talking to government departments so that these procedures are agreed protocol. In terms of Canadian ISP's receiving our notification to take content down when it is reported to us, if it is Canada-originated, it is effectively dealt with. If it is outside Canada a different protocol is used as explained above. A large percentage of images come from outside Canada. In 1999, 77% of content came from the US; that generated within Canada was far less; the same for 1998. It is a matter of what people are reporting to us. This is a reflection of Internet traffic and number of people using it. The US is big and 2/3 of traffic originates from there. I think the Canadian figure has gone down and the few noted are more of a reflection of the traffic of transmission in previous years. It is Canadian reporters who tend to look into Canadian sites; the Canadian proportion of illegal content was exaggerated, but I think it is about right now. The thing we claim but cannot prove or we believe we but cannot prove is that because our operation has improved people are encouraged to question illegal content in this country. That is an argument, but is an unproven argument for the effectiveness of this service. This is a working hotline and if the police are effective in the country of origin, then the whole system works.

However, there is problem of illegal content on websites from countries like Russia where we presume that the police are not effective in how to deal with the Internet or perhaps they are discouraged from dealing with the Internet by a bit of corruption. Yes, Eastern Europe is the worst place, though it used to be Japan where the law was not strong enough against child pornography. In 1999 the Japanese government passed a law against child sex and the phenomenon has reduced a lot. So those sorts of patterns indicate some kind of effectiveness.

ALEXIA: If a pornographic material exists on a server, who decides whether further action is needed or not, what criteria are used and what is the status of the decision-makers?

IWT: There is a diagram on our website and I think it is reproduced in the annual report. It is a diagram of what happens to our reports. Essentially once we have seen something and it is illegal, we are committed to doing something about it. The exact procedure will depend on where it is; once we have established something to be illegal we establish where the news originated from or the ISP involved or the website where it is registered. So it is not necessary just to have the main name; it could be dotcom, but we would look it up, and if it is dotcom, but it is registered in the address of a registrar which is locally based we will report that as much as we can. So we pass it on to the police for investigation and prosecution, which is the first step. So we contact Canadian police if it is Canada-based and to the National Criminal Intelligence Unit if it is necessary to pass it on the country of origin. Increasingly, we pass reports directly to other hotlines, particularly as a lot comes from the US we send a standard report over the Internet to the other Hotline in the States, because we find that this method is much quicker in getting there before the FBI or local law enforcement gets it. So it gets to the police in the quickest way as possible. The second objective is to get it removed if it is on a Canadian server. We have got no authority to remove it if it is posted overseas. But if it is only a Canadian server and it is posted by a Canadian service provider, which is one of our members we tell them to notify the culprit as to what to do. We are advisors to service providers so strictly our notification to them is an advice to them which says "we think this particular content is illegal and we advise you to remove it, but is their decision. We have worked hard at getting our advice accurate and getting accepted as generally correct. This is important because most Internet Service Providers pay us to advise them of illegal content, and they accept our advice and take action on it. The real authority comes in the sense that they know, according to the original deal, that if we have told them about it, then they are aware of the presence of allegedly illegal content, so that any protection they have from police prosecution is removed by the fact that they know it is there. And if they keep it they are taking risk of prosecution since they have got to defend the reason for keeping it. So that is how the authority issue comes in. What we found in practice is that most ISP's use systems that are automated for removal. We send them a standard mail and their systems automatically take it down. So that not only reflects their trust in our advice, but it also makes removal quicker, as once they see the report in terms of identification it is down within minutes. All Canadian ISPs are entitled to get our notifications, and a number of the major ones and the associations subscribe to us, and we are funded by their subscriptions. In other words, these are the bodies, which fund us. Canadian Internet Service Providers Association in a way covers most of the ISPs. LYNX is the body which has all the international backbone connection to the Internet. Hence, any body that has international connection to the Internet is a member of LYNX. So any ISP in this country is either a member of LYNX or is a customer of a member of LYNX.

ALEXIA: How much awareness does the public have about the availability of Hotlines, and through which media are they informed?

IWT: It is difficult to know exactly, but we have always felt it is important that people were aware of our existence and contact us. Obviously it is the purpose of our unit so that people get a means through which to report. The last survey statistics we had was about two years ago, about half way through our existence when some institutions did a joint review of our work and the consultants used a small questionnaire or part of a small questionnaire to see how much of the public knew about this. At that time 6% of the people they asked had heard of the IWT, but that was a bit misleading because that was a general audience, and when you narrow it down to those who use the Internet you have 20%, which we thought was not bad at that time although obviously we expected a higher percentage. We hope it has gone up a bit since then, but there are always a recurring number of incidents and it has become difficult to improve since then and we hope to do another survey. So I would hope that we start and we would try and maintain our momentum. We don't need to pay for it at this stage, but we will try and get as much coverage as we can in the media. We recently appointed a public relation person internally to take charge of media issues. With respect to the radio, we get a lot of interest from it and are consequently getting a lot of radio interviews. We also get a reasonable amount on TV coverage; probably only a couple of times in a year on network TV. But on local/regional stations and things like the CBC Service, we probably get something on about once a month as the phenomenon filters in. It depends on what is happening. If sensational issues like the W0nderland trials come up, we probably do about 20 news items a week, and it goes up and down. So that is one way of getting coverage. The other way is to encourage all ISPs, particularly our direct members, to publicize us with their own communication systems to their members and on their websites so that if someone has a problem with some sort of abuse, he turns to his own ISP. And if their own ISP advises them to contact us then we take over from there. However, they still find us and the number of reports keeps going up, but they are about the same pace, on the average.

Q: What about using leaflets? Do you hand out leaflets or put them in the libraries as a form of drawing attention?

A: No, we don't. We have a plan to produce posters, which would go to police station and schools. There are a number of developments to be undertaken. We are now in discussion with one of the major suppliers of software and hardware to enable us produce leaflets. Additionally, we will encourage them to print these leaflets and deliver them with their new PCs to customers. This is a big supply and that should cover about 30% of the national market. We will have that spread to other suppliers so that when parents buy PCs for their kids, they will have guiding leaflets. The main problem with child safety, as opposed to reporting illegal content or chat room safety, is we are always aware that generally parents are ignorant and kids know more than they do. So I think awareness is obviously reasonable, but we need to do another survey. In terms of press coverage and hits on our website, we now report all these in all our board reports, so if you look at the Chief Executive's reports, they are all now on our websites.

ALEXIA: What communication channels do you mostly employ to exchange information with other agencies?

IWT: Almost exclusively by e-mail. This is where we are probably different....The police are becoming more efficient in using the Internet. Ours is entirely by e-mail. There is an issue of confidentiality in the use of e-mail, and we have a policy, though we have not fully implemented it yet, where our e-mails would be encrypted to send our notifications to ISPs in this country and for sending messages to other countries. We have a very strong bar, with respect to child pornography, on actually sending data, and we discourage people from sending us pornographic material, because it is illegal to send these over the telephone wires, and because we are dealing with materials which are publicly available, when people tell us where they are we can find it ourselves. The same with the police, we don't send the police copies of pornographic material. We tell them where to see it, and the consequence of that is that when something comes to court we are practically never caught without evidence. We have always told the police where to find the item based on our own evidence, which is further substantiated by police raids and recovery of illegal content on the perpetrator's hard drive. Essentially, we communicate by e-mail solely in transferring information about child porn. Other information is relayed on our website for business only, for example on our meetings.

Analysis of Speech from Hotline Experts

Alexia, once again, stayed on to summarize what the Hotline experts said.

"Many issues were raised by Hotline officers. However, five major factors of relevance emerge. These are limitations due to prioritization of cases, limitations due to the source of the images, language barrier, co-ordination difficulties and financial resources."

ONLY MOST SERIOUS CASES

"Firstly, the respondents are of the opinion that because of limitations on service resources, they do not deal with every case, especially now that cyber porn traffic is growing. They confront the most serious cases only. This implies that for those cases termed less serious, control efforts are not made and perpetrators are allowed to continue with their activities."

"It was made clear that law enforcement agencies, including hotlines, are now faced with both traditional crimes and newly emerging computer crimes. However, with limited resources, there is a need to prioritize these crimes for action. In this sense, it would appear that not all preventative institutions, and for that matter all nations, will put emphasis on the same crime at the same time."

"Though it is wise to prioritize in committing resources to a cause, any thought of allowing perpetrators of Internet pedophilia to get away because of lack of adequate resources smacks of negligence. Secondly, the idea of seriousness can be relative and subjective, which can severely impede the control of the phenomenon in question."

Publicly Displayed Images

"Another important point is the fact that since Hotlines in Canada deal only with publicly displayed images as seen on websites, it is felt that an increasing proportion of images as appear in chat rooms, news groups and encrypted ones like those that circulate hidden in MP3 files are not within their remit. This also means that their work is severely limited. In the combat against indecent images of children on the Internet, the difference between publicly displayed images and hidden ones must be clarified. However, the two overlap on many fronts. The hidden ones are found in chat rooms, newsgroups and specialized websites, where predators know that indecent images are sited. Curiosity causes some novel and uninitiated users to stumble into these channels; however, for most experienced predators, they visit these sites with intent and by all means."

"There are various ways by which knowingly or not one can obtain indecent images on his screen. Examples are typing the wrong words into an Internet search site, scanning an e-mail and the chances of finding a couple of messages from a teenage temptress, innocently going into a chat room for other purposes and being approached by someone directing you to a porn site, or just being confronted with offensive material on your computer screen. The public, through the availability of hotlines, are given the opportunity to voice their concerns about that which they have stumbled across in the course of their legitimate use of the computer. In other words, though other areas of the Internet like the chat rooms are also public, it is observed that only people with special interests access files contained in these areas. Their clandestine interest in these files is such that they wouldn't be expected to be surprised to see indecent images of children, let alone to report them. However, law enforcement officers have some power to do surveillance work in some of the Internet areas, which are outside the jurisdiction of Hotlines. This aids in bringing the determined perpetrator to justice, and emphasizes the need for all agencies concerned to co-operate with and complement one another. Unfortunately, hotlines are not set up for images from chat rooms and other specialized sites to be relayed to them, though an innocent user could report on what he has seen. The truly concerned member of the public is not expected to pry into such sites, meaning that the area of jurisdiction of hotlines is limited."

"In view of such difficulty, our attention was drawn to the importance of foolproof and capable guardianship. Capable guardianship has evolved since the beginning of human history; from feudalism to the rise of the state and the proliferation of public institutions of social control, to the post-modern era in which employees of private security services vastly outnumber sworn police officers in many industrial democracies. Guardianship against conventional crime involves preventive efforts on the part of prospective victims, contributions by members of the general public or commercial third parties, as well as the activities of law enforcement agencies. As noted, it is often only when private efforts at crime prevention fail that law enforcement is sought and the criminal process is mobilized and, for example, the public is warned of special areas of the Internet that portray children being abused or of making such images available on the Internet."

"Technology can also enhance guardianship. It was explained that various technologies for detecting attempted intrusions of information systems. For example, alarms can indicate when repeated login attempts fail because of incorrect passwords, or when access is sought outside of normal working hours. Other anomalies that detection devices will identify include unusual patterns of system use, including a typical destination and duration of telephone calls, unusual spending patterns using credit cards, or trails of deleted files on hard drives and CD ROMs."

"Citizens' concern about the availability of undesirable content has given rise to the private monitoring and surveillance of cyberspace. Citizen co-operation can complement activities undertaken by agencies of the state. An example of collaborative public-private effort in furtherance of controlling objectionable content is the use of Hotlines."

Language Barriers

"Thirdly, with respect to enhancing preventative measures, the Internet Watch Tower has taken great strides with respect to reducing the effect of language barriers. For example, due to the possibility of language barrier for non-English speaking callers, the Foundation has installed translator software in its computer system. In addition, it has made it possible for callers to contact them through e-mails, on-line forms, telephones and letters. It has also made room for callers from different countries and directed them to the nearest home Hotline. The public has been made aware of the foundation's activities through radio, TV and national Newspapers. This awareness has also been created in Websites of member Internet Service Providers."

"In summary, in encouraging the emergence of a new tradition of responsibility for the regulation of illegal content on the Internet, it can be argued that Hotlines are very essential instruments. They can take on a central role within a self-governing system involving the state, media supervisory bodies, the Internet industry, including its users, not just as a channel of communication, but also as a means of evaluating problematic Internet content."

"The term 'Hotline', was interpreted as a connection between a sender and a receiver, where the connection is qualified by easy accessibility, high availability and an assured response system. Hotlines in the private sector are used by enterprises to offer direct access to "help desks" or related services dealing with consumer and client requests over the telephone or via communication services offered via the Internet. With respect to public services, Hotlines serve as a means to provide information, offering communication or services which can be used to initiate a particular action. In both realms, the term does not only connote easy availability and accessibility, but also means speeding contact with responsible personnel offering users opportunity to bypass frequently used or choked channels."

"Hotlines may just be links to an information contact that provides less further information beyond what is already displayed. On the other hand, it may stand for an elaborate system of receiving, processing, verifying, evaluating, deciding and finally acting on complaints. It may be operated on a purely automated basis, or have individuals or some organizations behind them. Generally, Hotlines are a means through which complaints by users are received about illegal material on the Internet, especially child pornography."

"Factors, which created awareness of Hotlines, were explained. One of the characteristics the Internet shares with other media is that users do get exposed to content that they may not have expected, which is not surprising to regular users. But when browsing, "surfing" or following suggestions from search engines, there is a tendency that any encountered page may contain unwanted material. While the mixture of the deliberately sought for material and the unexpected material constitute one of the challenges of the medium, taking advantage of the opportunity the medium offers is one of the most important tasks in Internet maintenance and makes the medium so important for the freedom to seek and gather information, to develop and to exchange ideas. A caution was made clear that exercising of any freedom online is not risk-free and that there is always the possibility not only of encountering material with which one strongly disagrees, but which is also deemed to be harmful or judged illegal."

"Another factor raised is the appearance of disorder indicative of the fact that public order cannot sufficiently be maintained, which in turn leads to more disorder. In the context of the Internet industry, the phenomenon of child pornography on the Internet implies a sense of insecurity of the medium because of doubts about the identity of communicants or content providers, the integrity of the data being exchanged and the assurance of children's privacy rights. It is in this situation that systems like Hotlines have been set up to maintain communication freedom."

"Hotlines have been seen as initiatives that could be instigated without legislation and that might provide an outlet for public complaints and an opportunity to devise procedures to deal with reports of illegal content. Internet Hotlines serve to support the Internet industry, law enforcement agencies and users in the identification of illegal content, particularly child pornography. Hotlines thereby assist in preventing the distribution of such content and contribute to the investigation of associated criminal acts. They can work alongside the efforts of law enforcement agencies in the fight against illegal content. Hotlines can also co-operate internationally more easily and more effectively than law enforcement agencies, which are generally bound by complicated and tiresome procedures. Hotlines offer users a reliable and immediate responsive point of contact to which they can report dubious content found on the Internet. Thus, they protect freedom of communication when they prevent governments from enforcing tight restrictions in response to public concern, or when providers blow issues out of proportion, in acting hastily to block a wider range of contents than it is necessary. This is particularly dangerous during periods of critical media coverage of sensational cases. Hotlines contribute to the removal of illegal content from the Net and help to strengthen trust in international networks. They demonstrate that their operations share the ethical concerns of Internet users and thereby increase trust on the Internet. Many people contact them not just about contents, which are clearly illegal, but also provide information about how to deal with harmful content."

"On the whole, Hotlines make a contribution to the social learning process within the Internet industry, and to achieve these aims, they have to maintain contacts with law enforcement agencies and Internet Service Providers and respond to complaints from users. Seen in the context of self-governing institutions such as law enforcement, rating and filtering systems, Internet Service Providers and their codes of practice, Hotlines may be defined as the communication channel for these institutions' response mechanisms. In other words, whereas law enforcement provides complementary approaches by way of regulation and private/public enforcement action and whereas rating and filtering provides technical and organizational means by which eventually users themselves can respond to their concerns, Hotlines are essentially means of communication, linking the user community to the institutions involved in these processes of self-governing."

"In summary, Hotlines are imbued with the ability to be accountable to the general public. They can also be found responsible for safeguarding civil liberties, for educating industry, consumers and government, for monitoring and evaluating developments and for effective responses They can prove trustworthy by establishing effective internal evaluation and quality assurance procedures, by keeping abreast with social and technological development and by promoting co-responsibility. Furthermore, the Internet industry can be reliable, as institutions like Hotlines are consolidated and managed to fit into the self-governing image. Reliable because users can have confidence that procedures will be followed accurately; and show transparency as users get to know who runs the Hotline and how it deals with reports."

Alexia then announced that a breakthrough has now been made and the culprit will be made public as soon as conviction and sentencing become imminent.

CHAPTER FIFTEEN
GRAND FINALE

A body was found by three teenagers at about 2:30 pm while scouting in a cave along the beach about a mile from the hotel occupied by the Morrison family during their holiday. The small girl was dressed in her morning gown with a tape covering her mouth and her tiny wrists tightly tied to a stony pillar with a rope. She had no pants on. The three boys quickly raised an alarm. The immediate mouth of the cave is frequented by visitors, but rarely do they venture deeper into it. Criminal Scene Investigators were called to the scene, who combed and carried out extensive examination of the area. They collected whatever trace evidence they could find including clothing, fingerprints, human hairs, blood traces and cigarette butts. Word quickly reached Alberta Police in Calgary.

Around 7 am, Detective Inspector Yaba Soul was having her breakfast when her cell phone rang. Yaba Soul has a Master's degree in Forensic Science from Edmonton University's prestigious centre for Forensic Studies. She has special interest in trace elements on dead bodies. She was assigned the case and told to fly from Calgary to Del

Soro immediately to work with the local agents. She went with two other special agents with 20 years experience. Though very tired, the moment they arrived the two agents were led to the cave for more forensic analysis while DI Soul went to the mortuary to study the body carefully. The girl was beautiful and may be between 3 and 5 years old.

The autopsy was done by Dr Papatowski, a respected Forensic Pathologist. He was Canadian-trained but lived locally as the Chief Pathologist. After an extensive analysis, he confirmed the age of the body at death as around four years old and concluded that she was raped and asphyxiated to death. At the time she was found, she was gagged with brown tape. During examination, cotton wool was found in her throat. She had been dead for five days. Further analysis revealed that she was made unconscious at the time of abduction with a quick-acting anaesthetic. However, she regained consciousness and struggled with her assailant when she was being raped. Materials found under her finger nails suggested that she scratched the murderer. The fact that the perpetrator left his mounted web camera behind would suggest that he was frightened by something and ran out in a hurry and in confusion. However, there was no fingerprint on the system. He wore hand gloves, also indicating that he planned the scheme meticulously, and that it was not a spur of the moment issue.

Before starting his mental health ordeal and subsequent visions, the Morrison family came down to Del Soro again to identify the body. Previous dental records made from X-rays compared perfectly with current ones. There was no doubt that the body found was that of Elsie Morrison. Two days later, the body was flown back to Calgary.

Del Soro, a Spanish Island in the Mediterranean Sea of just under 6000 residents, is not known for any serious criminal activities. Due to extensive media attention, the case became talk of town. It has always been known to be a Children's Paradise and for such a murder to occur would not only put fear within the peaceful residents, but it was felt that tourism would also be affected. Considering the target of this crime, there was speculation that the murderer would be a local who did this after chance meeting the family for a failed favour or someone who had known the family and had some score to settle with the victim's family. If the second guess were correct, then the murderer could possibly be a foreigner. In any case Del Soro was determined to track down the perpetrator and bring him to justice.

Consequently, a massive door to door search was conducted to interview residents and to collect mouth swabs for DNA analysis. None matched with standard database results on local people, as well as the analysis done on materials found under Elsie's fingernails. When it became clear that Del Soro was not going to yield any positive results, attention turned to the Calgary area in Canada. Interpol was also contacted. After five days, whoever committed the offence and was not a local resident would have run away from the Island; likewise, a normal resident in the face of such intense public reaction.

In Canada, a check of the Criminal Record database containing millions of fingerprints and DNA results yielded a clue, but it was inconclusive at this point.

Back in Calgary, DI Yaba Soul and her team were not ready to give up easily. Discouragement and frustration were setting in, especially considering the fact that there was a backlog of many murder cases that have not been resolved for a long time. She thought to herself: what are the chances that we can bust this one. Then remembering that Elijah Morrison was made fun of for waking up from his coma shouting anaconda, anaconda, she felt deep down that she was not going to conduct this business based on the normal scientific method alone. She was going to take into consideration the paranormal. After briefing her staff for consensus, she informed the police service and all citizens to be vigilant and report any suspicious behaviour as well as take a close look at tattoos of words and images on people, be they tramps, criminal suspects or convicted criminals in secure units.

It was 1 am on Sunday morning. Police was called to a public house about 15 km outside Calgary. A bunch of drunks were found in a brawl with broken bottles and knives and disturbing the peace. Some of them were bleeding profusely. One of the tramps was Alan Fiasco. He was bleeding seriously from the back of his head with the blood oozing down his back. An ambulance was called and those badly hurt were taken to the nearest hospital. On exposing his back to clean the blood and stitch the deep cut sustained, a huge coiled snake was found to be tattooed on his back with blood flowing over the snake's mouth down his back. It did not occur to anyone at first what they have found or stumbled on. The nurse, however, recorded everything she did and saw.

After her shift at 7 am, the nurse, Andromeda, went home and before reposing to bed to rest awhile she thought of having her breakfast while watching the morning news on TV. Detective Inspector Yaba Soul came on the screen to appeal to every one to be on the lookout for anything, tattoos or words indicative of a snake, anaconda or any Amazon valley creature. It suddenly struck the nurse that the man she worked on just before coming home could be a wanted person. She quickly called the police and directed them to her workplace. Blood samples were taken and DNA analysis done. Meanwhile, Alan Fiasco was asked to be retained for further questioning in due course, if need be. Five days of detailed analysis of all trace evidence including sperm found on Elsie's private parts matched perfectly with that of Alan Fiasco. Indeed, Elijah had a vision and he was not in a coma for nothing. Furthermore, it appeared the spirit of Elsie Morrison hovered over Alan Fiasco.

When he woke up the following day after being brought to the hospital and had sobered down, he enquired where he was and how he ended up in the hospital. After it was explained to him the circumstances, he was asked what kind of snake was tattooed on his back. He responded that he has always been curious about the Amazon anaconda, so he asked that to be tattooed on his back. It did not take long for the police to swoop on him and charge him for the murder of Elsie Morrison. The day was January 11th, the following year, exactly 6 months after she vanished. His first reaction was, "wait a minute, you must be joking here. I do not know what you are talking about."

A background check on Alan revealed the following: He was born on January 1, 1960 in Red Deer, Alberta, into a well-to-do family. His father was a top military officer and his mother was a nurse. As he grew up, all he heard was, "a job half-done is no work at all," and "in all areas of endeavour, try and be the best or with the best. Then, "there is no standing still, either you move ahead or fall behind." Alan was equipped to work very hard on whatever his hands found to do. He and his sister Isobel were cushioned from every form of difficulty. Their parents provided them with almost everything to make their lives very comfortable. The family home was open to family friend and relatives. Under these circumstances, Alan gained a lot of confidence, a sense of friendliness and generosity. At the least opportunity he would jump to someone's need. By the time he was in High School, he had already grown to be 6 foot tall and a big star in the ice hockey team. It was clear that he had the brain and the body structure to charm any girl. Professionally, he wanted to be a top oil tycoon. During his first degree at the University studying business administration, he met Clara, also a Red Deer resident, who was studying Computer Science in the same University, but a year behind Alan. Clara's father was also in the military as a top Naval Officer on HMS Noahsark, the latest high-tech naval ship. Her father was being flown to Ottawa for a briefing when the military helicopter crashed at sea. He did not survive. The bond between Clara and Alan became more cemented out of sympathy and growing love. Both successfully completed the courses and planned to marry two years later. It was clear in their interaction that they were deeply in love. There was no single occasion in her interaction with others that she would not boast of him. She would say to any man trying to chat her up, "my Alan is as tall and strong as a cedar tree, more handsome than Romeo and as constant as the Northern star." Whenever there was a misunderstanding or quarrel, Clara would cross her heart and say, "hey Alan, do not forsake the love of your youth." During the waiting period prior to the wedding, every opportunity to interact was ecstatic, memorable and heart-throbbing. However, right from the beginning Clara made it clear to Alan that sex before marriage was a no-go area. Each time Alan made any move to go beyond the boundaries, Clara would jokingly say, "you can touch every part of the succulent mango, but tasting would have to wait until after the wedding meal." Then Alan would ask, "when shall this be?" Pulling his ear, she would say, "businessman Alan must know after putting on my finger that sign of eternal love." They will then laugh and be on the move. Alan came to this bend several times, but Clara, deeply influenced by her Christian background resisted. Alan eventually understood her values and became determined to wait as their love became stronger and stronger. The only woman he had known very well was Clara, and was not in the mood to mess things up.

Alan took up a position as accountant trainee in a reputable accounting firm, while Clara became a computer science teacher, hoping that with such a profession she would have more time for her kids. The marriage ceremony was scheduled to fall on Saturday January 2. To be or not to be was the question. Just a week before the wedding, Clara and her mother were doing their last-minute shopping in a jeweller's shop when two gunmen, in balaclava, burst into the shop at about 4 pm. Clara and her mother were at the counter paying for what they bought when the two robbers held the store up, threatening to kill the shoppers if they did not lie on the floor. The man at the counter was ordered to hand over all that he had in the till. When he made a move to reach something under the table, he was shot dead in the head, as the assailants thought he was pressing an alarm bell to alert the police. In the melee, Clara and her mother made for the door. In the confusion, the gunmen started shooting randomly, with one bullet hitting the back of Clara's head. She was pronounced dead on the spot. The gunmen fled through another door. The much-awaited mango eluded Alan. His love was gone. But he took courage to go on in life. It took another year before he met Sandra at a Christmas party. At this point, though his job was going very well, his thought of Clara got him so depressed that he started binge drinking. Sandra was not aware of the extent of his depression. Could he love Sandra as much as he loved Clara?

After three years of marriage to Sandra, not only was Sandra incapable of conceiving, despite all medical intervention, but the couple realised that it took a long time during love-making for Alan to have an erection. There were two miscarriages, though. The family doctor diagnosed him as having a mild hypertension and he was put on medication. Alan was brilliant at work but his depression increased as he saw his dream of raising a family fall apart. Doctors warned him of increasing and serious high blood pressure. The situation came to a head when he realized that he had become impotent at a tender age. However, the exact cause of his impotence could be pinpointed. Sandra, who was a dress designer, decided to spend more time with her husband in anticipation that things would work out well for them. With time, she observed that Alan was not coming home at the expected time, and when he did come home, he would say he was tired and better be left alone for sometime either in the study room. Sandra would then go to bed alone, toss from left to right on the bed, gaze on the ceiling deep in the night wondering whether her husband truly loved her. Meanwhile Alan had two issues in mind, which he could not share with Sandra. Why he had become impotent and why Clara died. It was a mixed feeling. Was he still emotionally involved with Clara, and would not let her go? Deep in the night he would keep awake, drink alcoholic beverages, and silently cry himself to bed. Sandra would pretend to sleep as she watched her husband staggering to bed. He would not attend to counselling of any sort. He tried Viagra and other anti-impotent medication but to no avail.

Meanwhile, in the Newspapers and in the office, there was hype over Internet pedophiles and why they behaved like that. What he heard from a colleague was his unmaking. Some Internet pedophiles use pornographic images to attempt to bring their phoenixes from the ashes. That was a brilliant idea for Alan, in view of his situation. In the night when Sandra was in bed alone, he would remain in the study room to download pornographic images and imagine all sorts of things to see whether the phoenix would rise. However, nothing happened. Maybe it would happen if he visited children's playgrounds and swimming pools or the red-light districts of town.

Having worried and depressed to her tethers with Alan coming from work late and coming to bed late, she planned to stalk him for as long as she could afford by hiring a private detective. On this occasion, he was seen entering a nightclub about 30 km out of town and in a particular dress. As seen by the detective, he sat in the lounge looking around as somebody in expectation. Then entered a very young girl, who wore a make-up to make her look like an adult. Apparently she was merely a 14-year old runaway girl who lived in a home for teenagers with behavioural problems. After winking, he followed her into a room. It turned out that she was one of the girls who would lure a man to a room and when it was time to make love to her she would ask you to switch off the lights and go to the toilet naked for a pee detailing all sorts of reasons and experiences for which she wanted a man to do that. She would give the man a sign of readiness before coming out of the toilet. The plan was that she would empty all pockets and suitcases of valuables and quietly leave the room with the man's dress including his underwear. That was what happened to Alan. He did not have a second dress so he had to call reception for help. It was too late. The girl was gone, and no one could identify her. Being given a second-hand shirt, the detective saw him coming out on to the foyer. More pictures were taken.

The time was about 11:30 pm when he arrived home with a smile.

"You must have been very busy at work as usual, honey?" Sandra welcomed her inside.

"Yes, we are coming to the time in the year when we get deeply involved in auditing and other mind-boggling issues causing one to stay in the office for a long time," Alan lied.

"And why are you in a different dress from the one you took to work?" Sandra asked.

"Oh, during lunch time, I was heartily munching my pizza when it fell on my shirt and trousers. I took them to the dry-cleaners," he answered.

"That must have been very embarrassing," Sandra said.

"You must be hungry and tired. Perhaps you may want to shower and have some dinner before doing other things," Sandra added.

"Thank you," Alan ended the conversation. The following day was Saturday, and Alan lied to Sandra that he was going to check on the dry-cleaners at 2 pm. She then found a place to call the detective to come to her home at 3 pm with any pictures he had taken. When Alan came home late in the evening a fiery exchange of words ensued.

"You liar, have a look at these pictures and explain from which other planet they were taken, and what the hell were you doing in these scenes. Why do you dishonour me by going after children and maybe other sick women? If I do not take care, not only would you infect me with some dreadful disease, but you may also make me mad. I should have left you a long time ago, but I was patient. I am out of this house within a week," Sandra blurted out.

"That Saturday night he sat on his computer and continued with his sordid behaviour. He never came to bed. The following day he continued to drink and thinking that he was still sober enough, he took his car out for a drive, hoping to get away from all the rancour at home. Not only did he jump a red traffic light but he also ploughed into a mother and her three children who were crossing the road. He tried the brakes, but it was too late.

Fortunately, the speed was so reduced that two members of the family sustained only minor injuries. Their 12-year old boy was badly hurt and died a week later. The day before Sandra was to leave the house, the police called the home and decided to search the house for drugs and other pieces of evidence including the home computer.

Forensic analysis indicated that in addition to being charged with murder, he had also downloaded pornographic images of children. He was sentenced to a prison term lasting five years. DNA analysis and fingerprinting were completed and kept in a database.

It transpired that having become confused with his relationship with Sandra he became more and more involved in children for sexual satisfaction. Being cognitively distorted in his perception of children, he embarked on a life of sexual fantasy of children, which he reinforced by pornographic images of children. As he fantasized, he attempted masturbation frequently but gained no success, as his impotence situation was not resolved. This experience was repeated over and over and punctuated by stress and loneliness. He then decided to go live by looking for children with the intention of eventually sexually engaging with them personally. To achieve this he needed to overcome both internal and external inhibitors and child resistance. Internal inhibitors were disregarded under the influence of drugs, alcohol, psychosis, stress, repeated exposure to indecent images of children and minimization of any adverse effect on his victims through systematic desensitization. To overcome external inhibitors he decided to look for a child who had an absent caregiver, ill or powerless guardian, and someone who lacked social network/emotional support.

Then he would exploit an unusual opportunity for contact with the child. Neither of these activities was effective enough to raise his phoenix from the ashes. He became very frustrated. Having overcome any form of inhibitors, Alan then targeted other places where children could be found to talk to them or take pictures. He also looked up children on the Internet, believing that his behaviour was harmless and he would eventually be healed of his impotence and help reconcile with Sandra. His aim was to select a child physically or in the chat room and groom the child by spending a long time on this particular child in order to know enough about her, her family and her movements. In other words, he was building trust from helpless victims. This phase was also repeatedly punctuated with fantasy and manipulation of his genitals for possible erection. Eventually, he gained physical access to Kyla in an attempt to arouse himself with a child's help in the hotel. He did not know that the girl was as deceptive as himself, if not more.

Kyla was a 14 year-old girl, who appeared to be 18 years old. She was the only child of her mother's as his father died when she was two years old. Rarely did she receive love from her mother, who portrayed depression most of the time. Living ten blocks from Alan's house, he befriended her mother. Alan introduced himself as an amateur comedian. Kyla was unable to resist any kind of abuse, which was shrouded in a form of concern for her well-being because she was emotionally insecure and physically deprived or isolated. She believed Alan to be an established comedian in a position of trust and felt threatened if she should say what was going on between her and Alan. As he helped Kyla's mother financially, he abused the girl by touching her in several areas and took several pornographic images of her as he promised to help her become a model.

For these offences, he lost his means of livelihood and was sentenced to 5 years in prison. When his activities were exposed, and before sentencing he expressed stress, an intention to commit suicide and other forms of psychosis. However, there was evidence that he had ongoing mental health problems before committing the offences. His Barrister expressed these sentiments: "he should be considered on the basis of personality disorder." He added that, "it became clear to me during his psychosocial assessment that his personality traits, which are enduring patterns of perceiving, relating to, and thinking about the environment and oneself, became disordered. Clearly, he has appeared to be inflexible and maladaptive in the past, setting off this dysfunctional behavior."

The Prosecutor rose and defended the state thus: "Yes, the behavior of Internet pedophiles like Alan seems to tally with the characteristics of people with Antisocial Personality Disorder, which are callous unconcern for the feelings of others and a lack of capacity for empathy, gross and persistent attitudes of irresponsibility, an incapacity to maintain enduring relationships, a very low tolerance to frustration and low threshold for discharge of aggression, an incapacity to experience guilt and to profit from experience, a propensity to blame others, persistent irritability, general conduct disorder before, and irresponsible and antisocial behavior, and reckless. Alan appears to have exhibited all these traits.

"However, he must face justice as is expected. One major factor, which seems to be common with all these Internet pedophiles like Alan is that they are very deceptive and lead double lives. Whereas under normal interviewing conditions such perpetrators would confess to a couple of abuses, when faced with a rigorous evaluation with, for example, a polygraph and conditional immunity from prosecution for the disclosures, a method we employed in this case, they confess to many more abuses for which they would never have been convicted."

"Well-respected members of the community like him always got away free because they have been so good in putting up fronts that they have had public opinion swayed in their favor in times of apprehension for child molestation. It is well documented that it has always been very difficult for parents, close associates of perpetrators and some members of the public to accept that people with impeccable credentials and known responsible behavior have been caught abusing children. One reason is that human beings are easily fooled. Sometimes it is impossible to convince people that private behavior cannot be predicted from public behavior, and that kind, non-violent individuals behave well in public, but so do many people who are evil behind the scenes."

"Leading double lives, Alan and his friends depend on pre-planned niceness and likeability. They cultivate the ability to charm with good looks and to radiate sincerity and truthfulness. They camouflage their evil intentions by portraying extensive participation in public good causes. Many look angelic on the outside. Then unbeknown to the public, they would be abusing children at unsuspecting moments. In effect, a pattern of socially responsible behavior is followed in the sight of others to cause a drop in guard and watchfulness."

But what was the connection with Elijah Morrison's family? It turned out that, Chen Ping, having been saved after an attempted suicide got in touch with Alan, whose nickname was Anaconda and a cold-blooded child abuser. He had just been released from Federal prison a year after his 5-year custodial sentence. Unemployed, he was promised $50,000 with cash down payment of $5,000 given to him to stalk Elijah. He virtually stalked him for about six months and managed to obtain his itinerary. He had had mental breakdowns several times, influenced by cocaine and alcohol, but he steadied himself for the operation.

He confessed that he was approached by Chen Ping and offered $30,000. But after hard negotiations they agreed to $50,000 plus $5000 cash on hand and a return air ticket, which he agreed. Chen Ping's intention was that after abusing the child and murdering her on resistance, emotional damage or depression would cause Elijah to lose his job, just as he had lost his.

Anaconda followed the family to Del Soro and hired a house about a mile from the Morrisons' residence on the slopes, but making sure that he followed him wherever he went. Using binoculars, he was able to know more about his surroundings. One day when the family went out he got very close to the house to observe the doors and how to jump through any of the windows. He was able to know where Elsie slept because one day he kept 24 hours vigil with infra-red goggles and saw, by chance, Elsie looking outside her window for a brief moment. Then at 4:00 am on July 10th, he struck, after trailing the family since the previous day. He climbed into her room through the open window and knocked her off with an anaesthetic. He strapped her on his back and lowered himself down a ladder he had hired previously. The moon was bright, but he was very careful not to attract anyone. He sent her into the cave, undressed her and after sexually abusing her and taking several pictures at various poses, she came round and started scratching him in an attempt to free herself. Some of the pictures were sickening. There was Elsie lying on her front with her hand tied behind her and being buggered by an adult. She was also pictured with her legs wide apart and an adult's finger pushing her foot out exposing her vagina. Then an adult's erect penis is seen facing the girl's vagina. As dawn was approaching, and fearing that some fishermen may hear any noise, he had no choice to cover his trails but to kill her by snapping her neck. He was wearing a balaclava and plastic gloves. He realised the cave was deeper than he thought. He took her further inside, tied her body around a stony pillar, took more pictures of his necrophiliac behaviour, and ran out after hearing strange noises coming from inside the cave. In panic and confusion, he forgot his video camera, but since his digital camera was always around his neck, he took it with him. He was given a life sentence after being found guilty on this occasion. Chen Ping, realizing that he would be implicated successfully committed suicide this time. At last justice was done for Elsie, and Del Soro once again regained her peace.

Detective Inspector Yaba Soul and Alexia Denford became close friends and unfolded the news on TV and the Newspapers. They both became promoted. Bertha became pregnant again and got non-identical twins, a baby girl and a boy. She named the girl, Jochebed and the boy, Ezra. They grew to be very sweet children.

www.ingramcontent.com/pod-product-compliance
Ingram Content Group UK Ltd.
Pitfield, Milton Keynes, MK11 3LW, UK
UKHW022210230426
12048UKWH00016BA/751